DEPTH CHARGE

CAINE: RAPID FIRE BOOK FOUR

ANDREW WARREN
AIDEN L. BAILEY

DEPTH CHARGE

Andrew Warren
Copyright © 2018 by Andrew Warren. All rights reserved. This is a work of fiction. Any resemblance to actual persons living or dead, businesses, events or locales is purely coincidental. Reproduction in whole or part of this publication without express written consent is strictly prohibited.

Cover design by Onur Aksoy
aksoy.onur@iCloud.com

Please visit:
AndrewWarrenbooks.com

Please Join my Readers Group!

You might get a chance to read the next Thomas Caine thriller for free! You'll also get access to special sales, contests, and new release info...

Please visit
AndrewWarrenbooks.com
for more details.
Thank you.

AUTHOR'S NOTE

The events of *Depth Charge* take place before *Devil's Due*, when Thomas Caine is still a paramilitary officer in the CIA's Special Activities Division / Special Operations Group...

CHAPTER ONE

MACAU, PEOPLE'S REPUBLIC OF CHINA

Thomas Caine stepped from the shadows into the light. His emerald eyes were focused and intense. His SIG Sauer P226 handgun was raised and ready.

The spacious office was dim, lit only by the neon glow of adjacent skyscrapers. Blinking shafts of light beamed through the bamboo scaffolding that surrounded the building.

Most of the light came from a massive glowing billboard that adorned a nearby building. The luminous sign displayed the head and bare shoulders of a beautiful woman. Her skin was pale, and a bob of black hair framed her perfect cheekbones. Dark sunglasses masked her eyes. The o-shape of her mouth glistened with desire, and looked ready to reach out and kiss him.

Caine looked away from the gigantic portrait and advanced into the room. The fifteenth floor was devoid of people this late in the evening, as was the plan. But the man he had come to meet was also missing. That wasn't part of the plan.

It was too quiet. Too still. It felt wrong.

Another shaft of neon cut through the dark room. Caine spied a silhouetted figure, slumped over a desk at the far end of the office. Glowing lines of text scrolled across the flat-screen monitor in front of him. As Caine moved closer, he made out latitude and longitude coordinates. IP addresses. Ocean currents and satellite trajectories.

"Min?" whispered Caine, fearing the worst.

His instincts screamed. *Turn around*, he thought. *Walk away. The operation is blown.*

But he needed to know if Jasper Min was actually dead or merely incapacitated. Caine stepped closer. "Min?" he said again.

The man wasn't moving. He wasn't even breathing.

In the dim light, Caine could just make out a thick black pool, expanding under the corpse's twisted feet. Another shaft of light angled through the room, revealing the sticky fluid to be crimson red.

Caine stepped around the body. A red gash cut across the corpse's neck. Jasper Min's throat was slit from ear to ear. Caine touched the man's face with the back of his hand. The body was warm. A recent death.

"Min won't be joining us," called a voice from the shadows.

Caine whipped around and raised his firearm.

Three men in dark suits emerged from the darkness. Each held a QSZ-92 semi-automatic 9mm pistol, aimed straight at Caine's heart. Weapons favored by the People's Liberation Army and the People's Armed Police.

Assassins, Caine knew. *Professionals. I didn't hear them sneaking up behind me.*

The center man took a step into a shaft of light. The harsh glare revealed his features. His eyes were like two dark pools of murky oil. His head was large and bald, and his skin was as pale as the moon.

"A foreign spy caught red handed," he said in practiced English. "What should we do with you, Mr. Caine?"

Caine's emerald eyes blazed in the darkness. He glared at the man, but said nothing.

The moon-faced man grinned without humor. "Don't be foolish, Mr. Caine. Things can always get worse."

"At least we agree on something," Caine said with a shrug.

He slowly raised his weapon in surrender, then moved his finger away from the trigger and dropped it at his feet, keeping it close enough that if any of the three men went for it they'd be in Caine's striking distance.

And there's still my knife, he thought.

He wore a Strider SMF fighting knife, strapped in a sheath on his right leg. There was no way he was going to let himself end up in a Chinese black prison. The poor souls who entered such bleak, quasi-legal facilities were rarely seen again. They were tortured, abused, humiliated, and eventually executed.

There would be no outcome tonight where he was going to let these men take him, alive or dead. One way or another, he knew he would need his knife soon.

There was no point in denying their charges. He figured these men were intelligence officers of the MSS, China's Ministry of State Security. The organization was responsible for counter-intelligence, foreign intelligence and political security. The MSS had eyes and ears everywhere in China. If they were on to him now, they had probably tracked his every move for days, if not weeks.

Caine put out his wrists ready to be cuffed. He needed the men to get close. "Are you going to arrest me?" he taunted.

"Arrest you?" said the moon-faced operative. His voice held a condescending tone, and his lips curled into a sneer. "That is a Strider SMF knife you have strapped to your leg, Mr. Caine, is it not?"

Caine resisted the urge to look down. The knife was indeed hidden exactly where the moon-face operative said it was. He had been compromised even worse than he'd thought.

"You are former U.S. Special Forces, yes? Marine Raider Regiment, perhaps? They train their recruits to slit a man's throat with that very same weapon."

Caine said nothing.

"Poor Jasper Min. An honest programmer working for the PLA. An innocent man you corrupted with promises of money and a new life in the west. But his usefulness had run out, so you murdered him. We arrived too late to save Mr. Min's life, but at least the culprit was apprehended."

The operative looked from Caine to Min's corpse. "No, I have a better idea. We arrived just in time to shoot the culprit... while resisting arrest."

Outside, fireworks erupted over the Zhiang River. Caine heard faint music in the distance... A celebration of the latest casino opening in Macau's crowded gambling hub.

Adrenaline flooded his nerves. His instincts spurred him into action. *Now!* he thought. *Move!*

Caine ripped the flat-screen from Min's desk. Sparks flew as he threw it hard across the office. The moon-faced man grunted as it slammed into his jaw. Caine heard the snap of breaking bones.

He was running, sprinting for cover, before the man hit the ground.

More fireworks, greens and reds, blues and purple, lit up the velvet night sky. The pyrotechnics disorientated his foes, bathing their scowling faces in a dizzying array of colorful light.

The two standing agents squinted in the sudden bright lights, then opened fire. The bullets missed Caine by inches, whizzing past his head and shattering the glass ahead of him.

He leapt through the broken window without a second thought. As he flew through the shattered glass, he remembered he was fifteen stories above the ground.

The bamboo scaffolding, he thought. *Should break my fall...*

Unfortunately, he misjudged its width. He flew over the narrow planks, and plummeted into darkness. He was falling, tumbling through the warm night air. One, two, three floors rushed by... He flailed his arms, reaching out for the skeleton of bamboo poles to slow his fall.

On the fourth level his fingers finally gained purchase. His body whipped back towards the building. He hit the bamboo gangway with a thud, landing on his back. The air exploded from his lungs in a pained gasp. His muscles throbbed, and he felt like he had run face-first into a brick wall.

Again, fireworks crackled above him... Primary colors, drowning out the starlight.

Caine stumbled to his feet, felt the bamboo planks wobble beneath him.

Then the gangway collapsed...

He fell three meters onto the next gangway, groaned as further pain seared through his legs and back.

Again he staggered to his feet. Before he could take another step, the first MSS operative swung down, slamming a kick into his chest.

Caine staggered backwards. His eyes watered and his head spun.

The operative came at Caine fast with a barrage of kicks and punches. The strikes were fast and powerful... the practiced maneuvers of a trained martial artist. Caine blocked and parried, barely able to keep the attacks from landing on his face and chest. His arms and legs took a beating as they deflected the force of the blows.

As sparkling yellow and orange fireworks lit up the sky, Caine caught a glimpse of the impassive woman on the billboard. The gigantic black circles of her designer sunglasses gazed over the melee below.

A second kick thudded into Caine's chest. The pain and the force of the blow sent him reeling backwards. His flailing arms grabbed a loose bamboo pole. He bent the flexible wood backwards as he staggered away from his attacker. He released the pole, just before it snapped.

With a loud twang, the tensed bamboo pole sprang violently back. The operative cried out in pain as it struck him in the face.

Caine seized the moment of distraction, and charged at the man.

They collided and tumbled over the edge of the scaffolding.

Caine reached out and grabbed a dangling rope. As he fell, the line tangled around his leg and flipped him upside down. He jerked to a halt, suspended far above the busy Macau streets.

The operative was not so lucky. His scream faded to an echo as he plummeted to the streets below.

Caine felt air rush past him. The crack of gunshots thundered through the night sky.

As Caine swung in a wide circle, he craned his neck and looked up. The two MSS operatives leaned over the scaffolding. They were shooting at him, without a care for the people in the streets. He heard the screams of pedestrians rise up as they spotted the violent scene unfolding above.

Guess the falling body got their attention, he thought.

Caine swung back and forth, unable to control his motion as the bullets whizzed past.

The second operative's weapon clicked empty. The man leapt down three levels, landing on his feet like a cat. He quickly reached the rope entangling Caine. He drew a knife and began to slash at the fibers.

Caine swung close to the scaffolding, but not close enough to grab the bamboo poles.

He swung out again.

The rope strained, its strength dissipating as the twines were cut one by one.

Caine reached up and pulled down his pants leg. His fingers wrapped around the pommel of his knife, and he drew it from its sheath. He aimed at the operative and his arm snapped forward, hurling the weapon through the air. The hundreds of hours he'd practiced throwing knives paid off. With a wet thud, the razor sharp blade struck the operative in the neck. The wound gushed blood, painting the wall behind him with a crimson splash. The man didn't have time to scream as he fell backwards. He was already dead when he hit the gangway.

The rope holding Caine slipped and he fell another few meters.

The scaffolding creaked as he swung closer to the building. He reached out, grabbing a bamboo pole just as the rope gave way.

The tension hissed out of the severed rope, and the tangled coil slipped from around his feet. Caine clambered onto the gangway of the next level. He looked up.

The final operative stared down at him. His jaw was bruised, and his mouth still gushed blood from the impact of the monitor. He bellowed a curse in Chinese and swung towards Caine, dropping one level after the other.

Caine spun around, and tugged at a vertical support pole until it came away. Then he kicked at another. The wood splintered as he battered it with more blows. As it snapped in two, he raced along the gangway, and kicked another. Then another.

A series of snaps and creaks filled the air. Without the supporting poles, a half-dozen gangways fell, crashing down towards him. The operative screamed as the scaffolding collapsed around him.

Caine sprinted along the plank, struggling to avoid the falling beams before they crushed him to a pulp.

The gangway underfoot tipped down at a steep angle. Caine lost his footing and began sliding downwards. As the bamboo skeleton continued to crumble, the angle became steeper, until it was almost vertical. He was tumbling, falling until he came crashing down on top of the operative.

Together they crashed through another gangway. They were clawing, punching and kicking at each other. Like the other MSS operatives, the man was skilled in martial arts. He kept coming at Caine with swift, deceptive feints and attacks. His face was a bloody mess and his jaw looked shattered. Shards of bamboo were impaled in his back as a result of his fall. But his injuries didn't slow him down. All Caine could do was keep his arms up to defend his body. He tried to keep his limbs loose so his attacker didn't trap him in a lock and snap a bone.

A kick in the thigh sent Caine crashing down.

In desperation Caine reached behind him, searching for a weapon. His flailing fingers wrapped around a snapped bamboo pole.

His attacker launched into another volley of kicks and strikes. His fist swung toward Caine's throat, aiming to crush his airway.

Caine jabbed the splintered bamboo shaft up like a spear, impaling the operative as he lunged forward.

The man stopped in his tracks, gasping in pain as the jagged tip pierced his heart and lungs. He fell to his knees. His face turned even paler as a stream of crimson blood flowed through the hollow bamboo shaft.

Caine scrambled back just fast enough to avoid getting the man's blood on him. Then the operative tumbled sideways, and fell into the Macau night.

The bamboo structure groaned and shuddered again.

Before Caine could react, the gangway tipped and he was sliding.

He struggled to gain purchase, a foothold, anything to stop him falling to his death.

But he only fell a couple of meters, then landed on his feet.

He had already reached street level.

CHAPTER TWO

Caine's emerald eyes glanced around the street. Hundreds of pedestrians surged through the crosswalk, moving towards the hotels and casinos. Slim trench coats covered the wide-eyed women's glitzy cocktail dresses. Men wearing dinner jackets and expensive suits stared at him in shock and disbelief. Caine knew it was only a matter of time before one of these people took his photo, compromising his covert status. But so far, the crowd near him seemed too surprised to even reach for their phones.

He stepped forward as the remaining bamboo scaffolding collapsed into a heap behind him. People screamed and backed away from the wreckage. A cloud of dust filled the air as he walked away.

Caine wasted no time blending with the crowd. As a *gweilo*, a ghost man with a Caucasian complexion and bright green eyes, he stood out. He needed to put some distance between himself and the crime scene. He heard sirens wailing in the distance, drowning out the explosive fireworks. Too many people had seen him. His description would soon be broadcast on all the police channels.

Whichever way Caine turned he felt watched. He glanced up at the mysterious model on the towering billboard. The dark pools of her sunglasses and her sleek naked shoulders loomed over him, fifty meters from neck to scalp. Her giant pouting lips looked ready to kiss him. He had an uncanny notion she was watching over him.

A light rain shower suddenly fell from the sky. The droplets painted the streets with a slick, black sheen. Caine turned and walked at a brisk pace, matching the speed of the foot traffic. The dense crowd offered concealment, but it was impossible to see more than a few meters in any direction.

The fireworks continued to burst above. The crackling pops and explosions sounded like gunfire. Caine's eyes darted around the mass of people, scanning for any threats, his senses on high alert. He had to get off the streets as soon as possible. He stepped into the road to cross.

A BMW Mini Cooper pulled up fast, then screeched to a stop. It reversed until it was directly in front of Caine.

The passenger door swung open.

A young, slim Asian woman in her twenties sat behind the wheel. Her hair was tied back in a short ponytail. She wore jeans, blue canvas shoes and a striped t-shirt. There was no one else in the car.

"Get in," she said in English.

"Do I know you?" Caine asked.

The woman did not smile. There was a trace of fear in her voice. "I know you. And so do the men chasing you."

Too convenient, Caine thought. *This has to be a trap.* The sirens wailing in the distance grew louder. Closer.

"Quickly," the woman hissed, her voice a panicked whisper. "It is only a matter of time before they find you."

Caine made his decision.

"We'd better get moving then," he replied in a low, hard voice. He kept his eyes fixed on the woman as he ducked through the door. Despite the risks, the offer of a ride seemed preferable to evading the authorities on foot.

The young woman stepped on the gas, and maneuvered the Mini Cooper into the heavy night traffic. They sped out into a sea of blinking tail-lights and neon buildings. The rain grew more intense, spattering the windshield with a percussive beat. Caine didn't mind. The inclement weather made it harder to spot him in the car.

Caine looked his savior up and down. He thought he might have recognized her, but he wasn't sure. Perhaps her face was in one of the many profile reports he was supposed to digest back at Langley. Maybe she'd sat in on MSS/CIA cross-table negotiations. But she didn't strike him as an MSS operative.

She turned her eyes from the road for a moment and smiled at him. She was pretty, with shoulder-length dark hair, a slim figure, and she was of medium-height. Caine sensed she was nervous. Her smile looked forced, and her eyes had a pensive, haunted gaze.

"So, what's the plan?" he asked casually.

There was no doubt in his mind this woman knew exactly who he was and why he was in Macau. What he didn't know was if she worked for the Ministry of State Security, or some other interested party. It was also possible she was working alone. If he were a betting man, he would have gone for the second option.

She continued speaking in English. "I wanted to talk to you earlier, Mr. Caine, before those men took an interest in you. When they came to kill you, I thought I might have missed my opportunity."

Caine nodded and looked back to the road. They had pulled from the narrow, shop-lined streets onto the multi-lane Avenue Marginal Flor de Lotus. They sped past a row of shimmering hotels and casinos. The towering buildings disappeared into the rain and misty clouds above. Their architecture resembled a cross between ancient Chinese fortresses and gleaming skyscrapers.

The sirens and the police were far behind them now. After a few minutes the young woman pulled the Mini Cooper up to the Morpheus, one of the flashier hotel casinos in Macao. The modern building was shaped like a gigantic letter 'O', and its shimmering glass reflected the rainbow of neon lights surrounding them. Unlike most buildings, the Morpheus contained no internal support walls or columns. Instead, the glass exterior was wrapped in a freeform geometric exoskeleton. The interlocking white rods gave the structure its strength and rigidity. The building's warping curves and twisted glass made it look more like an alien organism than a decadent casino.

The woman darted the Mini Cooper into the parking garage. A valet driver took her keys and chattered to her in Cantonese. Caine didn't speak the language, but he assumed the man was asking for her room number. Then Caine and the woman exited the car and stepped into the building's palatial lobby.

"My room is on the eighth floor," she said quietly. "We can change there."

"We?"

"We need to talk, Mr. Caine. Your description will have been broadcasted widely." She nodded towards a mirrored column near the elevators. "There, why don't you secure yourself a fresh set of clothes before we head up?"

Caine noticed several suit bags hung on a rolling rack, no doubt returned from dry cleaning. He made sure no one was watching, then grabbed three bags off the rack as they walked past. The elevator chimed, and the doors slid open. He entered the car, the mysterious woman at his side. She tapped the elevator's control panel with her key card. The doors closed and the car ascended, speeding them up to the eighth floor.

"Eight, the Chinese number for fortune and prosperity," Caine said with a smile. "I hope that's a good sign."

"Who knows?" she replied, staring at the blinking numbers as the elevator slowed to a halt.

Once in her room Caine made a quick search of the sleek, immaculate interior. The modern room was decorated in deep red and black hues. Once he was satisfied there were no hidden attackers, or weapons the woman might use against him, he laid the three garment bags on the king-sized bed.

The first bag contained an Italian Zenga two-piece charcoal suit. Two business shirts in his size, and three neckties, hung beneath the luxurious suit. The garment's fabric looked expensive, probably worth thousands of dollars. He began to change.

"Are you going to tell me who you are?" he asked as he slipped on the charcoal trousers.

She shook her head. "Not here." She took a short black cocktail dress from the wardrobe and laid it on the bed next to Caine's new clothes. She slipped out of her canvas shoes, jeans and tee shirt. With her back to him, she slipped off her bra and dropped it on the bed.

Caine couldn't help but admire her slim figure. The room's soft lights highlighted her curves, transforming her body into a chiaroscuro of pale flesh and deep shadows. She slipped into the dress, wiggling as she tugged it over her hips.

Caine removed a pair of freshly polished black dress shoes from one of the garment bags, and slid them on his feet. Bare-chested, he entered the bathroom and checked himself in the mirror. Luckily, he'd suffered no serious injuries to his face from the earlier altercation. He patched up the cuts on his muscular torso and arms as best he could, using a first aid kit the woman brought to him. When he looked presentable, he threw on one of the white shirts.

"You scrub up quiet well," she said, watching him from the door of the bathroom.

Caine looked her up and down. She had transformed completely, looking every bit a sophisticated and elegant woman. "Is this supposed to be some kind of date?"

"You could say that."

Caine returned to his old clothes and collected a contact lens case from the pocket of his pants. He unscrewed the case, and popped the two lenses onto his eyes. He turned and looked back at the bathroom mirror. He too had transformed his appearance. His natural green eyes were a dead giveaway. The brown contacts made him less striking, but that was exactly what Caine needed tonight.

As the woman finished her makeup, he ran some grooming cream through his thick hair to flatten it down. Then he slipped on the jacket, along with a skinny argyle-patterned tie. Checking the mirror one more time, he was satisfied he looked the part of a rich businessman. He bundled up his old clothes and weapon holsters, ready to dispose of them on the way out.

"Where to now?" he asked.

"The casino, Mr. Caine. What else do you do in Macau?"

CHAPTER THREE

Caine and the woman stepped into the hall. He found a laundry chute and disposed of his clothes. His pistol and knife holster went into a bin on a room service trolley.

Within minutes they were inside the casino lobby. The vast chamber of marble and gold was packed with guests and staff. Every surface was polished to a sparkling sheen. A ring of fountains launched sparkling jets of water up from a shimmering pool. An array of strobe lights made the falling droplets appear to hover in mid-air.

Ethereal ambient music played from hidden speakers around them. Looking up, Caine saw Chinese women in silver and gold bodysuits, swinging from wires attached to the domed ceiling. Colored orbs and spheres spun around them in a slow orbit.

They found a bar. Caine ordered a James Boags lager, an Australian beer he'd discovered on a recent mission. His companion asked for a diet coke. Caine understood why she wanted to talk here. It was not unheard of for the MSS to bug rooms in the casinos. The music and crowd noise of the lobby would muffle any surveillance equipment that might be monitoring them.

He calculated how long they had before the MSS would track his movements here. He guessed they were good for half an hour. After that he would be pushing his luck. But before he left, he needed to understand who this woman was and what she had to offer.

"Well, now that we're enjoying a drink, are you going to tell me who you are?"

She sipped her coke, then spun the straw in her glass with her delicate fingers.

Caine sensed her unease. Before he could prod her again, she turned and looked him in the eye. "It's not who I am that's important. It's what I can offer you."

Caine raised an eyebrow. "What is it you think I'm looking for?"

"I know why you are here, Mr. Caine. You're trying to figure out how the PLAN is hacking into your NRO. How they are subverting your submarine tracking satellites."

Caine nodded. PLAN was an acronym for the People's Liberation Army Navy. NRO was America's National Reconnaissance Office. The latter operated America's network of defense and spy satellites. They had indeed been compromised, and Caine had been ordered to find out how and why.

She sipped her coke again. "Jasper Min promised to provide you with evidence of this, for money. But I can assure you, he never had the clearance or the access to do so."

Caine sipped his beer and hoped his blank expression masked his concern. Whoever this woman was, she seemed to know too much about Caine and his mission. China was flexing its military muscles in the South China Sea. They were constructing artificial islands, enforcing military and economic pressure on neighboring countries. The United States' ability to understand PLAN submarine movements, especially their long-distance nuclear vessels, was vital. Complicating matters, NSA, CIA and NRO cyber-specialist teams had recently identified intrusions on the NRO's supposedly secure server network. All evidence pointed back to the PLAN as the hackers. Caine's mission was to terminate those hackers, with extreme prejudice. But first he had to identify who they were.

He had thought of denying everything, but decided that was just wasting time. She obviously knew far more about him than he did about her.

"I'd be more inclined to believe you if I knew your name," he replied.

She took another sip of her drink, and gave him a pensive glance. "I guess you'll find out eventually. My name is Su Liao. I'm a civilian programmer with PLAN. I work on their submarine navigation systems."

Caine forced himself to keep his expression blank, despite his surprise. "Quite a risk you're taking, Ms. Liao. The MSS won't tolerate someone with your security clearance chatting with someone like me. Especially not after what happened earlier."

Su's eyes were wide and dark. He saw them glisten in the casino's shifting lights. She looked away for a moment, and dabbed at them with her napkin. "You're right, I'm taking a risk talking to you. But it would be an even greater risk for me to do nothing. My life is in danger. Or it will be, very soon."

Caine drank more of his beer. "And you think I can help you?"

Su reached into her purse, hugging it close to her body so no one could see what she was doing. She withdrew a data stick, and held it in her slim fist for a moment. Then she sighed and dropped it into Caine's waiting palm. "What you'll find there are the routes taken by all PLAN submarines in the last three months. You can cross check it with your NRO SIGINT."

Caine pocketed the memory stick. SIGINT was jargon for Signals Intelligence... information gathered by satellites, electronic communications, phone and text message tapping. It would be easy to verify if she was telling the truth.

"Why are you giving this to me?" Caine asked. He already suspected where this conversation was headed, but he had to be sure.

She finished her coke. "In two weeks I will be in La Paz, for the

Latin American Defense and Security Conference. That is the best opportunity for me."

"Opportunity for what?"

She stared at him like he was mad. "To defect, of course. I wish to come over to your side, and work for the CIA."

"Defect? You're serious?" Caine was even more suspicious now than he had been earlier. Chinese rarely defected or turned double agent. Their cultural and family ties were usually too strong to break. The CIA had been trying to recruit Chinese assets for decades without much luck. But if Su Liao was legitimate... Caine realized he might have stumbled into the intelligence coup of the decade.

"I'm very serious, Mr. Caine. If you agree, I will need you to stage my death, and do so convincingly. In return, I'll show you exactly how the PLAN is attacking your spy satellites. I can also help you hack into our submarine navigation system without being noticed. I coded in a backdoor access point, one only I know about."

Caine finished his beer. The waiter asked if he wanted another, but Caine shook his head.

He thought about what all this meant, what this woman was offering. The ability to track the movements of every Chinese submarine in real time, anywhere in the world... It would give the U.S. a significant advantage in power struggles growing between the world's two largest economies. He was about to ask more but Su was already standing, ready to leave.

"Don't follow me. We've been seen together long enough. You need to get out of the country, fast. The MSS have been onto you for weeks. It is only a matter of time before they find you. They will kill you when they do."

"How do you know all this?"

"I've been forced to work with the MSS. I helped them plant false information trails to lead you into tonight's trap. The plan almost worked. I'm glad you are still alive Mr. Caine, but if you're not out of China in the next twenty-four hours, I don't think you'll ever leave."

Caine didn't say a word. He stared at her for a moment, trying to guess if he was being played. He knew the subtle tells that could give away a lie or falsehood. But the woman didn't cross her arms or look away when she spoke. She was doing a commendable job of hiding her true emotions, but Caine sensed she was terrified.

"You said you were forced... Forced by who?" Caine asked. "The same people who are going to kill you?"

Her eyes darted around the room. "No more questions. La Paz, two weeks. We'll speak then, and only then." She pushed her empty glass across the bar, and stood up. "Thank you for the drink."

She turned and walked into the crowd, clutching her tiny bag under her arm. Caine watched as the sequins of her dress reflected the spinning lights above. Then she was gone, lost in the shifting bodies of the casino crowd.

CHAPTER FOUR

HONG KONG, PEOPLE'S REPUBLIC OF CHINA

Caine wasted no time extracting himself from Macau. A moored speedboat was waiting for him at a local marina, paid for and registered under a false name. Once on the water, he killed the boat's lights and donned his PVS-7 Gen 3 Night Vision Goggles. The pitch-black ocean glowed bright green through the lens as he raced across the water. The trip took no more than a couple of hours. Caine only made it into Hong Kong territorial waters just as the morning sun rose over the South China Sea.

Even at this early hour, commuters, red taxis and double decker buses packed the humid streets. Glowing neon signs blazed in the dim morning light. Skyscrapers cast their long shadows over the traffic below.

As he walked through the crowded streets, Caine performed a surveillance detection routine. He varied his walking speed, or made abrupt stops to tie his shoelaces. He made sudden changes of direction, pretending to window-shop in the stores along the sidewalks. After two hours of walking, Caine felt certain no one was following him. Only then did he make his way to the CIA's Hong Kong Station.

The CIA's center of operations in Hong Kong was inside the United States' Consulate General building. Like all embassies, the location was considered sovereign territory. It offered those inside diplomatic immunity. But Caine knew he couldn't just walk through the front door. The MSS kept the building under constant surveillance. Like all spies, Caine valued his anonymity. So he chose another route.

He entered via one of several discrete entrances spread across the Central District. The tunnel was hidden behind a false wall, in the men's bathroom of a cathedral in Cheung Kong Park. Caine followed the long dark passage until he reached another false stone wall. He pressed a stone in the wall, and it slid open. Next, he keyed his passcode into the secure steel-plated door revealed behind it. Only then did he enter the field office proper and U.S. territory.

The U.S. Marine manning this entrance nodded when he recognized Caine. Following standard procedure, he insisted Caine pass through the metal detector and sign in.

Five minutes later Caine stepped into the CIA's Hong Kong operations center. A collection of video screens covered one entire wall of the large room. The screens displayed satellite images of Hong Kong and China. Various blinking icons represented assets and other targets, tracked in real time. Dossiers of assassins, terrorists, and other persons of interest filled one of the glowing screens.

Caine was dismayed to see a news article from the South China Morning Post on another screen. FOUR MURDERED IN CHINESE GOVERNMENT BUILDING read the headline. It went on to mention that a Western foreigner was wanted for questioning in relation to the murders. The article included a blurry photo of the back of Caine's head as he disappeared into the Macau streets. Caine breathed a sigh of relief... His face could not be seen in the photo.

Caine scanned the other faces in the ops center to get a feel for their mood. Dozens of analysts wearing headsets tapped at their keyboards. Their faces lit up in flashes of dull greens and blues from their flat-screen monitors. When one of them looked up and noticed him, her expression was a mixture of surprise and relief.

Caine ignored her gaze. He headed towards two women engaged in hushed conversation in the center of the ops room. They were a pair of black shadows, silhouetted against the wall of glowing satellite images.

The woman on the right was Jezebel Yan, CIA Station Chief Hong Kong. She was tall and gangly, with long black hair. A sharp fringe of bangs accentuated her stark, expressionless face. Caine knew a little about Yan. A career CIA case officer, Yan had a law degree from Harvard, and a masters in international terrorism from the University of Baltimore. She was also fluent in at least five Far East languages.

After proving herself as an intelligence analyst, Yan was promoted to field operations. She had pulled off successful missions in Indonesia, Thailand and the Philippines. And if the rumors were true, she had quashed at least one military coup in a country friendly to the United States.

It was whispered that Yan's successes had earned her the ear of the Director of the CIA. Caine had taken heed of those rumors, and kept on her good side as best he could. It was difficult for a man like him. His decisions in the field could have long-term impacts on national security, both good and bad. When things went bad, he knew he made Yan's job even harder.

The woman on her left was younger, in her mid-twenties. She was tall and fit, with fiery red hair tied in a ponytail. She wore a slim-fitting two-piece business suit. Despite all that had gone wrong, Caine found himself smiling at the sight of her.

Rebecca Freeling... A rising Case Officer at the CIA who was following in Yan's footsteps. Caine had worked with her before, most recently in Yemen. She too was being groomed by the higher ups, and had been transferred to work with Yan. Rebecca had insisted on bringing Caine along as her man on the ground. Together they were tasked with a very specific mission: identify and eliminate the hackers attacking NRO satellites. And stop whoever was systematically murdering U.S. agents inside mainland China.

Now that Caine had blown his cover, both their futures in the Far East might soon come to an end. It was common knowledge in the office that Caine and Rebecca were more than just friends. He knew that wouldn't help their case.

For months now, Caine had been debating how to handle his relationship with Rebecca. Before Yemen, he had been struggling to keep his distance. He was assigned to a high level deep cover mission, an operation Rebecca knew nothing about. The fallout from Yemen had delayed his deployment. But sooner or later, he knew he would have to disappear, leaving no trace of his activities or whereabouts. He had promised himself that he would use this extra time to cool things down, to put some distance between them.

It was a promise he had broken. If anything, they had grown even closer. But every day, the guilt that gnawed inside him grew stronger. He knew he was being selfish. The longer he waited, the more he would hurt her. But no matter how hard he tried, he just couldn't seem to make himself let go.

Rebecca noticed Caine before Yan did. She turned to him and shared an understanding look. She walked away from the senior woman, her heels clicking across the tile floor. As she passed Caine, she brushed her hand against his. Caine felt a spark of electricity as their skin touched.

"She's furious, Tom," Rebecca whispered in his ear. "Play it cool."

Caine nodded. He paused, waiting until Rebecca had stepped out of the ops center before he approached Yan.

"Thomas Caine." Yan folded her arms and tapped her foot. "I thought you'd be smart enough to have exfiltrated yourself from the country by now," she said, scowling.

Caine shook his head. He knew Hong Kong was the safest place in a thousand miles in any direction for him to be right now. Their laws covering espionage were fairly lenient. And their rules of engagement prohibited physical harm to all foreign intelligence officers. But he wasn't going to argue the point.

"I couldn't, ma'am," he replied in a low voice.

"And why the hell is that?"

He held the data stick Su Liao had given him. "Because of this."

CHAPTER FIVE

Forty minutes later, Caine, Rebecca and Yan sat in the field office's SCIF... The Sensitive Compartmented Information Facility. Their meeting room had no windows, and armored steel plates reinforced the walls. Air vents and ducts were protected by sound masking devices. Most telling, there was only one way in or out of the facility. This was as secure as it got, and there was a good reason to use the SCIF. What they were about to discuss was for their ears only.

Three linked computer terminals allowed access to Su Liao's data stick. The terminals were isolated from any network, ensuring the device couldn't infect the CIA or Embassy systems. For added protection, a technical intelligence officer scanned the data stick for malware, spyware and viruses. Once he confirmed it was clean, Caine and the others began sorting through the various files it contained.

"I have to admit, this intel appears credible," Rebecca said, her eyes glued to her screen. "I've cross checked the data with Naval Intelligence, the NSA, NRO. They all confirm this is the most accurate intelligence they've ever seen on Chinese submarine movements."

"I told you," Caine said, looking up at Yan. He could see the data from her screen reflected in her glasses. "Su Liao was scared. Whatever's driving her, this intel is the real deal. And this is just the tip of the iceberg."

"You still need to be out of the country tonight." Yan looked up and shot Caine a stern glance. "Look Caine, I know good intel when I see it. This is great work. But after tonight, you're blown. You can't work in China again."

Caine nodded. In the last twelve months, twenty CIA agents operating in the region had vanished. A few had been arrested. The others had been murdered in mainland China, and the semi-autonomous region of Macau. It seemed the Chinese felt they carried enough political, economic and military might on the world stage to avoid repercussions. They were striking back against espionage conducted within their borders. And they were doing so with extreme prejudice. If last night's encounter had gone differently, if Su Liao had not intervened...

You could have been number twenty-one, he thought.

Caine spoke in a calm, level tone. "With all due respect, Ma'am, I can still operate in Bolivia. I can still bring Su Liao in."

Yan shook her head. "The MSS know who you are. We'll be lucky to get you out of Hong Kong alive. Their operatives will be alerted to you now. Everywhere. Even in Latin America."

"Surely the MSS won't come after Caine in Hong Kong," Rebecca offered. "With the special laws here, the diplomatic incident that would cause—"

"There are other ways, Freeling," Yan countered. "They'll send Triad hitmen," she said, referring to the criminal syndicates dominating Hong Kong's organized crime scene. "They've worked with the gangs before. Quite successfully, I might add. As long as he's here, there's—"

"Fine," Caine interrupted. "I'll return to Washington tonight. I'll take one of our military flights out of the country. But in the meantime, let's assess this opportunity."

"I don't see why you need to be involved." Yan's remarks were again addressed to Caine. She adjusted her glasses, and leaned back in her chair. "You've brought in actionable intelligence. Others can take it from here."

Rebecca twirled a pen in her hand. Her eyes darted from Yan to Caine. He couldn't help but notice how stunning she was. She was cool and confident in the presence of two agents with many more years of experience than her. Rebecca had been with the CIA less than five years, recruited straight out of Princeton with a major in political science and a knack for languages. In a short span of time she had risen high within the ranks. Few agents her age could claim that level of success so early in their career.

"Jezebel," she said in a thoughtful voice. "We have to handle this delicately. Liao reached out to Tom. If we change handlers now, it might spook her."

Yan considered Rebecca's suggestion. To her credit, the CIA Station Head was not prone to clouding her judgment with emotions. Caine hoped she would remain unemotional until they decided what they should do next. "That may be. But this could also be some kind of sting operation. Targeting the two of you. A fresh team seems prudent."

"It's possible, of course." Rebecca's voice held a conciliatory tone, but Caine knew she would not have agreed with anything Yan had said so far. "This is a classic risk-reward assessment analysis. The risks might be high... and Tom and I both know what we signed up for. But the rewards... If Liao is legit, we might be sitting on the biggest intelligence coup in decades. We don't want to lose her simply because we denied her Tom as her contact."

Yan didn't smile. She looked downright frustrated and angry. Emotions were getting the better of her. "What are the possible scenarios, worst case?" she asked of both of them.

"The worst case—" Caine began.

"The worst case?" Rebecca interrupted. "This could be an

attempt by the PLA to get an asset inside our nuclear submarine program. Or another of our intelligence agencies."

Yan took a moment, leant forward, and said with a nod, "Well done Freeling. That's exactly what I'm afraid of."

"There is one aspect you might have both overlooked," Caine said in a quiet, thoughtful voice. The two women ceased their discussion and turned to him. He glanced at them both, then continued speaking. "I made some calls earlier. CIA Kashgar Station. They gave me a very informative briefing on Su Liao's background."

The two women paused as they remembered their geography. Kashgar was China's most western city, built on the edge of a desert near the borders of Tajikistan and Kyrgyzstan. It was once a major trading center on the old Silk Road, in the remote and sparsely populated Xinjiang Province. Kashgar was about as far away from Hong Kong as one could be, and still be inside China's borders.

"Well, what did you find?" Yan snapped.

"Su is Han Chinese. But she was raised in Xinjiang Province."

"Why is that important?" Rebecca asked.

"For a start, most Han immigrate to Xinjiang. Not the other way around."

Caine didn't need to explain that the Han were the largest ethnic group inside China. They held all the power in the country. Twenty percent of the world's population was Han Chinese, making them the largest ethnic group on the planet. But they weren't the majority in Xinjiang Province. Many Han Chinese were being 'encouraged' to resettle in the western province. In reality, it was an effort to dominate the ethnic landscape, reducing the power base of the local people, the Uyghurs.

"So?" Yan demanded.

"Ma'am, Xinjiang is suffering about as many state-endorsed human rights abuses as Tibet. Hundreds of thousands of the local Uyghur Muslims are imprisoned in State-run internment. 'Reeducation' camps, for speaking up against the Han 'occupation'. They're being cut out of the economy. Their businesses are being replaced by

Han enterprises. Their situation is so bad, Uyghur separatists are waging a covert war to break away from China."

"You think I don't know this?" Yan did nothing to hide her annoyance at Caine's unwanted political assessment of a remote province. "I still don't see the connection?"

"Ma'am, Su said her life was threatened. I believe I now know why. Six months ago, Su's parents were arrested by the Chinese authorities. They were incarcerated in one of those Uyghur internment camps."

"You said they weren't Uyghurs?"

"They aren't. But her parents could be sympathizers. Which means they'll face the same kind of 'reeducation'."

"I see what Tom is saying," Rebecca jumped in, catching up with Caine's train of thought. "The timing of her parent's arrest coincides with the commencement of the PLA hacking of the NRO. Su Liao could be involved somehow."

"It gets more compelling," Caine continued. "Kashgar Station recently intercepted a communication authorizing the execution of Su's parents."

"And were they?" Yan asked. "Executed, I mean?"

Caine grimaced. "We don't know. We have to presume so. If they were, it happened in the last couple of weeks."

For a moment Yan and Rebecca said nothing as they processed this new information. Then Rebecca broke the silence. "You think Su was coerced in some way, to do something illegal? And now that her usefulness has run out, the Chinese no longer need her parents as leverage?"

Caine nodded, "Which makes Su a loose end. And I think she knows it. With her parents dead, she has to assume she'll be next."

"That's a compelling reason to defect," Rebecca offered.

Yan stared at Caine over the rim of her glasses. "Or it could be an elaborate cover for a sting operation that's going to ruin all our careers!"

Caine stared Yan down, "It's possible, ma'am. But this is the intelligence gathering business. When has anything ever been certain? Every move is a risk, but we still need to play the game. The potential rewards are too great to ignore."

The color drained from Yan's face. "That's what I'm afraid of, Caine."

The desk phone rang. Yan answered it.

After a short, terse conversation in Cantonese, the call ended and she hung up. A sour look crossed her sharp features.

Yan looked up at Caine and Rebecca. "We have to cut this meeting short. The head of MSS Hong Kong is here, Caine. And he wants to discuss your fate."

CHAPTER SIX

Chen Fa Li looked too foppish and manicured to be an MSS operative. He was dressed in an expensive-looking suit, with perfect Savile Row-style tailoring. Under the suit he wore a crisp striped shirt with thick gold cufflinks. His fingernails were clean and perfectly polished, as were his brogue shoes. His hairstyle was straight out of the 1940s; a sleek part on the left side of his face.

Everything about his appearance screamed wealth and sophistication... A Westerner, a corporate trader. But of course, he was none of those things. Chen was a man who looked nothing like what he actually was.

That's what makes him dangerous, Caine thought.

Officially, Chen worked out of the Liaison Office for the Special Administrative Region of Hong Kong. His office coordinated the Chinese Communist Party's visible influence on the autonomous region, thanks to the agreements left in place by the British before their departure in 1997. But everyone in the CIA knew Chen Fa Li was a senior MSS operative. He wielded considerable power inside and out of the world's largest intelligence organization. Chen also only visited the CIA in person when matters were grave.

Yan and Chen talked for several hours inside Yan's glass bowl office. They spoke in rapid-fire Cantonese. Caine couldn't hear any of their conversation, not that he could understand it anyway. The thick glass walls of her office were soundproof.

Rebecca's attempts to spy on the pair from her work cubical next to Caine's had been more successful. She was better at languages than Caine, and had studied Cantonese since her reassignment to Hong Kong. Caine spoke Japanese and Spanish well, and was conversational with Arabic and French. He had tried to learn Cantonese and Mandarin, but with little success. The intricacies of Chinese languages had so far eluded him.

But Rebecca had another advantage as well. She could also read lips.

"I think you're going to be okay," she whispered. "So long as you're out of the country tonight."

Caine nodded. "I guess that's good news."

She glanced over at him. "You know you shouldn't even be up here," she added.

Caine narrowed his eyes as he stared at the Chinese man through the glass. "You're probably right. But I want to get a look at Yan's opposite number. Besides, he has no way of knowing I'm here."

"You're pushing your luck, and you know it."

He sensed a pensive look in her eyes, and her voice sounded strained. "Rebecca, what's wrong?"

She looked away, glancing over at the other CIA operatives and analysts. Everyone else was busy tapping away at keyboards in other cubicles.

"Everything," she whispered. "Everyone knows about us."

Caine was stunned. He had not been expecting that response. Early on when their relationship had been casual, they had kept it secret. At the time Caine had been fine with it. But now they were seeing each other all the time, working together day by day.

It made letting go even harder.

"It was going to get out eventually," he whispered back.

She scowled. "It's not that simple any more, Tom. What we do affects each other now. You're out of Hong Kong. So where does that leave me?"

"You mean in your career?"

Rebecca nodded.

Caine wasn't sure if he should feel anger or guilt.

Once again she looked away.

"Look, Rebecca," Caine mumbled. "You know I don't want to mess things up for you. If this is a good post, maybe you should stay. Maybe—"

"No!" She finally looked back at him. Her eyes were filled with longing. "I don't want that at all. I just don't…"

Her voice trailed off. Caine felt another pang of guilt, but he didn't know what to say. He thought back to their last mission together, in Yemen. When they both had thought he only had hours to live, they had almost expressed their true feelings for each other. Almost. Caine had kept his emotions in check. So had she. Now, despite his better judgment, he regretted that.

"Why don't we go somewhere?" he finally said. "Take a few days off, get away from all of this."

"Where?" she asked. "How?"

"I don't know," he muttered. He glanced around the office. "But taking a break from all this bullshit can't be a bad thing."

Before Rebecca could answer they were interrupted by Yan and Chen, as the pair stepped out of the glass office. Yan shook the smug Chinese operative's hand. After a few brief words, she guided him towards the exit.

But Chen was not so easily deterred. He glanced around the office, then made a beeline towards the cubicles.

"Damn," Rebecca hissed. "He's heading straight for us." She turned to face him, her eyes wide with concern. "I'd swear he didn't see you… it's like he knew you would be here."

Caine shifted in his chair. Rebecca had been right. He had pushed his luck. "Well, I'm blown anyway. I guess we'll see what he has to say."

Chen walked up to them and flashed a brief, unconvincing smile. "Mr. Caine," he said, speaking excellent English. He gave a polite bow, but his tone was terse and with a hint of anger. "You inconvenienced us tonight. Three of my top men, dead. How am I going to explain that to Beijing?"

"Sorry to hear that, Chen," Caine responded. He didn't bother to get up from where he sat. "But you seem to be a clever man. I'm sure you already have a story prepared... but of course, I wouldn't know anything about it."

"Well, we will see, Mr. Caine." He laughed, but no one joined him. Then suddenly he was serious and cold again. "It is good that we are meeting in Hong Kong, Mr. Caine. The laws regarding our mutual occupation are somewhat lax here, for the time being at least."

Caine smiled. "You have laws against working in an embassy?"

Chen uttered another brief laugh. "An amusing joke, Mr. Caine. But please believe me. If this meeting had occurred in mainland China, I'm afraid I would be forced to have you arrested on suspicion of murder and industrial espionage."

Caine offered a slight bow in return. "Don't your people have a saying, 'a wise man adapts himself to circumstances—'"

"—as water shapes itself to the vessel that contains it,'" Chen finished. "Yes, that is one of ours." Chen smiled with his teeth now. "I prefer a different proverb. 'If you are patient in one moment of anger, you will escape a hundred days of sorrow.'"

Caine nodded. "Those are words I try to live by, Mr. Chen."

Chen gave another small bow. "As do I. Perhaps we are more alike than I gave you credit for. At any rate, I will say goodbye now, Mr. Caine. Out of respect for Ms. Yan, I will not hinder your exit from Hong Kong. I suggest you leave quickly. And for your sake, I very much hope we do not meet again."

He turned and exited the area. He walked at a swift pace, as though he had urgent, more important business elsewhere.

Once he was out of earshot, Yan crossed her arms and glared at Caine and Rebecca. "You still don't think you're being set up?"

"Let me get out of the country first," Caine answered soberly, "before I answer that one."

CHAPTER SEVEN

SOUTH CHINA SEA

Captain Zhao Jianyu stood proud on the deck of his Type 093 nuclear submarine, the *Hai Long*. He admired its sleek design and modern details. This was his submarine. He commanded it. He held absolute power over every aspect of the vessel and the crew.

Even before his commission, Zhao had made it his business to know every detail possible about the 093. The new submarine was far superior to its predecessor, the Type 091. That model had suffered from poor reactor shielding, among other problems. That single design failure had left hundreds of 091 crewmen riddled with cancer, or suffering from other symptoms of radiation poisoning. By a stroke of good fortune, Zhao had been restricted to commanding diesel-powered submarines while the 091 was in operation. His manipulation of Communist Party officials saw him promoted to nuclear submersible command when the new model rolled off the production lines.

This was Zhao's third mission commanding the *Hai Long*. The Type 093 was a prototype, and the Americans knew nothing of its existence. The sleek and deadly submarine displaced seven thousand tons of water when submerged. At one hundred and ten meters in length, and with a beam of eleven meters, the *Hai Long* was the deadliest new weapon in the PLA Navy's arsenal.

The propeller system had improved since the 091, reducing the risk of tracking by American and Russian submarines. The nuclear reactor gave the 093 unlimited range, so it only had to surface for food or to replace air scrubbers. Zhao's favorite features, however, were the vessel's six torpedo tubes. He would need every weapon at his disposal for the risky mission that lay ahead.

Only minutes earlier, Zhao had received his orders from Southern Theater Command in Zhanjiang, Guangdong Province. PLA hackers had secured a back door into America's National Reconnaissance Office. They were secretly 'cleaning' satellite imagery, removing any records of the Chinese submarine fleet operating in the Pacific Ocean. Within the hour, when the data cleaning process was complete, the *Hai Long* would go dark. It would follow the prearranged route across the Pacific to Los Angeles, California. Then it would turn north, heading up the American coast to Seattle. Finally, it would return home, never once appearing on the NRO's surveillance network. If the Type 093 remained undetected from start to finish, the mission would be deemed a success. The might of China's latest generation nuclear submarine fleet would be unquestionable.

That was the official mission. But Zhao had other plans.

He took a deep breath as he surveyed the brilliant blue waters around the surfaced submarine. The tropical air of the equatorial Pacific Ocean felt warm and fresh on his skin. He ran over the details of his plan one last time in his mind. His lips curled into a grin.

He was about to become very rich.

But before he departed on his self-appointed mission, he had one final problem to resolve.

As if reading Zhao's mind, three of his loyal sailors dragged a struggling man up on deck. His face was swollen and bruised, the result of repeated beatings. His wrists and ankles seeped blood where he had been tightly bound. He wore only his pants and a singlet. Both were stained with blood, sweat and urine.

Zhao nodded as his men threw their captive to the deck. If any of them recognized the prisoner as Wang Hong Fei, the Political Commissar of the Central Military Commission, they gave no sign of it. They treated him as they would treat any enemy prisoner of war.

"You will pay for this, Zhao," the beaten man bellowed. His voice swelled with defiance, despite his beatings. As he spoke, Zhao glanced at his split lip and blackened eyes. The once powerful man before him now looked pathetic. Impotent.

"When the Communist Party hears what you did to me—"

"They will never hear about it, Wang Hong Fei," Zhao snapped, his voice booming with the deep, commanding tone of a military officer. He gave the prisoner another scornful glance. Wang was one of many useless political pests that filled the ranks of the party. Commissars, bureaucrats... Parasites. Men like Wang plagued the PLA, reporting on anyone who showed even the slightest inkling of disloyalty to the great cause. The zealous sycophancy of the commissars blinded them to true genius. They were nothing compared to real men of vision and innovation.

Men like Zhao.

Commissars like Wang didn't make China great. They held their nation back, trapped it in the stagnant mindset of the past. All for their own petty benefit. They were not the future.

"Are you threatening me, Captain?" Wang demanded. "I swear, I'll make sure—"

Zhao laughed, amused that the Commissar still thought he held even a scrap of his former power. "You could have been very rich, Wang."

"That is not what China is about. You're paranoid, Zhao. You've gone mad!"

"Are you sure about that?" Zhao took a notebook from his pocket. It was Wang's. The tiny notebook was filled with the man's scrawled 'political observations.' Wang had guessed some of the details of Zhao's plans, and noted them all in his little book after deciding they were treacherous. He had believed his notebook was well hidden. But on the *Hai Long*, Zhao wielded ultimate power. No secrets could be kept from him, and nothing could remain hidden long.

"I've read what you have said about me, Wang," he said, flipping through the pages of the notebook. He looked down at the battered captive sprawled across the deck. "Did you really think you could hide this from me? On my own ship?"

Wang's eyes grew wide with surprise. For the first time, Zhao sensed fear in the man. Finally, the message was getting through.

"You're deviating from your orders, Captain," Wang shouted. "You are jeopardizing the mission given to you by the Central Government!" Suddenly, for no sane reason, Wang staggered to his feet. The bruised and bloody captive made a desperate lunge towards Zhao. But before he could even swing his fist, three of Zhao's loyal sailors battered him back to the deck and pinned him down.

"Zhao," he screamed. "Soon everyone will know… You are a traitor to China!"

With a casual flick of his wrist, Zhao threw the notebook into the choppy ocean water. He watched Wang again, saw the fear grow in the man's eyes.

Zhao was enjoying this. "You forget, Wang, that I am very well connected to the Minister of Foreign Affairs. He is my cousin through my wife's family. And as they say, blood is thicker than water. They will believe me when I say it was a tragic accident."

Wang stopped struggling. His face paled.

Zhao chuckled. "You look like you've seen a ghost, Wang. Perhaps your own?" Zhao knelt down, staring the terrified man in the eyes. "Finally, you understand."

"You can't—"

"Yes Wang, I can. A military submarine is a dangerous place for a civilian like yourself. My crew is loyal, Wang. They follow me out of respect… something you know nothing about. Their reports will say the same thing. You were last seen heading up to the deck, sneaking out for some fresh air without telling anyone—"

"No!" Wang's mouth contorted into ugly shapes. What was about to happen was finally sinking in. His destiny led nowhere, except to a cold and wet oblivion. "Please—"

"When the order to dive was given, no one knew the tragic circumstances—"

"You can't kill me." His words were almost sobs.

Zhao knew he had to push a little farther. The man still believed he could talk himself out of his predicament. Zhao needed to push until he broke completely. Nothing else would give him satisfaction.

"I am a Political Commissar of the Central Military Commission," Wang blurted in fury. "You cannot threaten me and expect no consequences—"

"No one realized you had not returned. Not until hours later. Hours, Wang. By then, it was too late—"

"Please," Wang begged. Then, like a switch had been flipped, his words turned to blubbering cries. He broke down suddenly, as tears flooded from his eyes. His body shook and trembled.

Zhao smiled.

This was the moment he had been waiting for. The moment when he could experience the sheer, raw terror of another man. Wang knew with absolute certainty he was about to die. Nothing in Heaven nor on Earth would save him.

Zhao closed his eyes, and took another deep breath. He savored the man's fear and pain, as he had savored the fresh air earlier. The suffering of others gave him power. It was almost like a spiritual awakening. He wished he could hold onto that feeling forever.

When Zhao felt he had drunk his fill of Wang's fear, he nodded to the crew. It was time to dive.

It was time for a man to die.

With sadistic laughs, the sailors threw Wang Hong Fei over the edge of the submarine.

Wang cartwheeled into the water, landing with a loud splash. He bobbed to the surface, treading water. Once again, he was begging and sobbing.

Zhao grinned as he savored the last moments of the man's naked terror. They were at least a hundred kilometers from the nearest island. Too far to swim. If Wang didn't drown first, sharks would find him soon enough. The man had no hope.

Wang tried to swim back to the *Hai Long*.

Zhao unbuckled his sidearm from its holster. He fired several shots into the water near Wang. He was careful not to hit the terrified man. He didn't want to quicken the demise of the bureaucrat who had been a thorn in his side for so long. The bullets nipping at the water had their desired effect. Wang paddled frantically, swimming away from him. His begging cries became muted and distant, muffled by the water lapping at the submarine's hull.

One by one the crew returned inside. Zhao stayed above, staring at Wang as he drifted further into the endless void of water. He inhaled the fresh air one last time.

In five weeks, each man on his crew would know greater riches than they could have ever dreamed of. Zhao Jianyu himself would become one of the wealthiest men in China. And then no one, not even the doddering old fools in the Communist Party, would ever be able to touch him again.

Success, Zhao knew, now came down to one thing; the PLA's whore of a programmer doing her job. It was up to her to fake a believable path across the Pacific and back for the *Hai Long* to follow.

He shook his head, realizing he had become lost in his thoughts. Wang was no more than a tiny black dot now, bobbing on the distant horizon.

Zhao ducked into the entrance and went down below. Within minutes, the deadly submarine vanished beneath the waves.

Its long, secretive journey had begun.

CHAPTER EIGHT

BALTIMORE, MARYLAND, UNITED STATES

Five days since their expulsion from Hong Kong, Caine and Rebecca had yet to formulate a plan to extract Su Liao from her MSS minders in Bolivia. The complicating factor was convincing the Chinese Liao had died during her defection. With just under two weeks to plan, the clock was ticking... they were under the gun.

They had been working sixteen-hour days, wracking their brains for a solution. Rebecca had been surviving on little more than black coffee, and Caine's diet had deteriorated into a steady stream of take-away meals. By five o'clock on the third day Caine suggested they take a break. Exhaustion wasn't helping, and neither was avoiding downtime. He offered to make her dinner at his place. A night off, to relax and regroup.

Rebecca agreed, but reluctantly.

At first Caine believed her frustration was with their lack of progress. But now he suspected it was because Rebecca blamed him for what had happened in Hong Kong. Because of him, she had lost an opportunity to work under one of the best station heads in the

CIA. Her frustration was affecting everything. She was more critical than normal. Her demeanor was cold. They didn't joke like they used to, to relieve the tension. The last five days had not brought the contentment Caine normally felt in her presence.

He hoped tonight would be different.

Caine enjoyed Asian food, so he decided to cook a Thai dish, a chicken and peanut Panang curry. As he stirred lime juice, pineapple, coconut milk and Thai basil leaves in a large pot, he felt his jangled nerves begin to unwind. The smell of the fresh ingredients had a calming effect on him. He soon found himself enjoying the simple task of creating a meal.

As he checked on the jasmine rice, Caine realized this was the first time in his adult life he had cooked for someone else. He had never gone to this much effort with any of his past girlfriends. He took a sip of a cold Sapporo beer.

Rebecca's different, he thought. *You're lying to yourself if you pretend otherwise.*

The doorbell to his sparse but modern apartment chimed. Rebecca was earlier than she said she would be. Early didn't bother him. He was looking forward to spending time together that didn't revolve around work.

When he opened the door, a crestfallen look crossed his face.

Rebecca was nowhere to be seen.

Standing in the door was a muscular, barrel-chested man. He had a scraggly beard, and stood a few inches taller than Caine. A curl of thick, sandy-colored hair fell across his pale blue eyes.

"Thomas Caine!" the man bellowed, holding up a six-pack of Coronas in each hand. "Thought I'd drop in and tell you the good news."

For a moment Caine said nothing. "Jack Tyler?"

"I passed, bud! I've officially joined the band. Paramilitary Operations Officer, CIA Special Operations Group. Man, those unit entrance exams were no joke!" Tyler paused, noticing Caine's surprised stare. "Hey bud, you gonna invite me in or what?"

Caine stepped aside and let Tyler into the apartment. "Ah, congratulations Jack. But I'm kind of expecting someone else tonight."

Tyler's expression turned serious. "Oh, sorry man. You working?"

"No, not exactly."

"Well, good thing I brought extra beer." All grins again, Tyler made himself at home. He fell into one of Caine's leather lounges and popped the lids off two beers with a knife he pulled from his pocket. "When your friend gets here he can celebrate with us."

"She," Caine corrected him.

Tyler cocked an eyebrow. "So that's why you're acting so cagey. Look at you, Caine. Got the lights turned down low in here, cooking a romantic dinner. I think I need to meet this girl. Make sure she's not running a honey trap on your ass, kid."

Caine sighed. The last thing he needed was for Tyler to find out about him and Rebecca, along with everyone else. He knew she wanted to downplay their relationship. "Actually, it is a work meeting. Need-to-know-only basis, I'm afraid."

"In your own apartment? My friend, you could be bugged. And I should know. I just finished audio-surveillance training at The Farm." When he saw Caine wasn't budging, he chuckled. "All right, relax kid. Join me for a quick beer and I'll get out of your hair. I owe you one, for recommending me to the program. And you owe me for saving your lily-white ass in Yemen."

Caine was about to argue when his phone rang. He recognized the number immediately. Rebecca's new cell number.

"Hi," he said, holding up a finger to silence Tyler.

"Hi Tom," Rebecca answered.

"How are you this fine evening?" The pre-arranged code phrase indicated that someone was listening to his end of the conversation. If he was alone, he would have asked, 'How are things today?'

"Right," she said. She sounded distracted.

Caine sensed something in her tone. A distance he didn't like. "What's up?"

"Something's come up. Work. I can't make it tonight."

Caine's heart sank.

When he didn't answer, she said, "Tom, I'm flying out in an hour. Last minute op."

Caine tried to keep his face impassive. He didn't want to give Tyler any idea of the emotions he was experiencing right now. For the first time in their long but casual relationship, he felt he and Rebecca were not growing closer. They were slipping apart. "I guess you can't tell me where you're going?"

"No Tom, I can't. You know how it is. But when I get back, why don't you and I grab a bagel, from that stand you like in Harborplace?"

"Sound's good," Caine said, masking his relief. She was off to Great Britain. The risk to her would be low in the democratic, stable and allied nation. He wouldn't need to worry about her.

"Sorry, Tom. I hope you didn't go to a lot of trouble with dinner?"

"No," he replied. "Haven't even started. We'll take a rain check."

"I'd like that," she said with longing in her voice. Then, in a professional tone, she added, "We still need to finalize that other op. I'll be back in two days. We can pick up then. You should take some time off until then. I think we both need it."

"Sounds good. Keep safe."

"You too, Tom."

The call ended.

Tyler was up on his feet handing Caine a beer.

"You got limes, bud? Can't drink Mexican beer without limes. Damn, whatever you're cooking smells good. Is that Thai?

Before Caine could stop him, Tyler was in the kitchen. "Well all right! If I'd known the CIA offered cooking classes, I would've trained in that too." He spooned out two bowls, one for him and one for Caine. "Look, I get it. A beautiful woman standing you up hurts as bad as a gut shot. Sorry to say, I've felt both more than once. But you get the consolation prize, kid. Me."

Caine shook his head and gave up any thought of kicking Jack

Tyler out of his apartment. He took a beer and didn't bother with the lime. He popped off the cap, and drank down half the bottle without stopping for breath.

"Jack, would you stop calling me kid?" he muttered when he finished. "You're what, two years older than me?"

Tyler took a swig of beer and sighed. "It's not the years, kid. It's the millage. So where's your girl off to? London?"

Caine stared down the former 1st Special Forces Operational Detachment-Delta soldier. Tyler had guessed correctly. "What makes you say that?"

Tyler swallowed some of his food "Hey, this is really good." He washed it down with a long sip of beer. "Not much of a code. Grab a bagel. G.B. ISO alpha-2 country codes. It wasn't too difficult to figure out."

Caine stared at him for a moment, then shook his head and laughed. He spooned some curry into his mouth. He had to admit, Tyler's skills of observation and lateral thinking served him well. He would make an excellent officer. "You didn't just turn up here for no reason, did you Jack? Guys like us don't operate like that."

"Damn straight," Tyler said between mouthfuls of curry. "Except in this case, I did. After the shit you pulled in Yemen, my interest in the SOG got to me. I figured, why should you get all the fun?"

Tyler took another sip of his beer and grinned. "Look, I know I can be a son-of-a-bitch sometimes. And I know there were plenty of times my attitude almost got me kicked out of the program." He pointed at Caine with the mouth of his beer bottle. "But you put in a good word for me when I needed one."

Caine smiled. Jack Tyler had gone above and beyond the line of duty when he helped Caine during a dangerous operation in Yemen. Jack had shown initiative in the field and coolness under fire. The man had taken out dozens of armed terrorists without breaking a sweat. He had saved Caine's life more than once on that op. Afterwards, they moved on to new missions within their respective groups, but Caine had kept an eye on the Delta Force operative. Later, Caine had approached Tyler and asked him to join the CIA's Special Activities Division's Special Operations Group, more commonly known as SAD/SOG. He was glad Tyler had made it through his SOG training. Not many candidates did.

"I heard you didn't know when to keep your mouth shut," Caine said through a grin.

Tyler grinned back. "Guilty as charged. Someone's got to show those pencil necks they don't know everything about the field. But I swear on my grandmother's grave, I just came 'round tonight to thank you, and celebrate. Mind if I grab seconds?" His held up his bowl. It was already empty.

Caine nodded towards the kitchen. "Help yourself."

He did.

"So, what's bothering you?" Tyler said, returning with his bowl piled with more food than the last serving. "I mean, besides your date blowing you off. You look like somebody just shot your dog."

"I've got an op I can't make work."

Tyler shrugged, nonplussed. "Alright. Let's spitball some ideas."

Caine sipped his beer and thought about the confidentiality of the operation in La Paz. He really shouldn't be discussing anything with Tyler. But he could do with some help, a fresh set of eyes. He could read Tyler in later if he had too. For now, so long as he didn't give any specific details, it wouldn't hurt to get another opinion. Hell, Caine needed one.

"I've got to bring in a double agent, one who is being closely watched by her masters. But I've got to make it look like she dies in the process."

Tyler finished his beer and opened one more for each of them, even though Caine was still drinking his previous one. "Well shoot, that's easy bud. Used to do that all the time with informants in Colombia. Drug lords down there will kill fifty men on a whim as soon as they hear the word 'snitch'. We had to make a lot of people look like they were dead when they were singing to the DEA."

Caine raised an inquisitive eyebrow. "How did you do it?"

"Three man team, a van, a highway, and a big payout to the local morgue and police. Worked every time. Classic rock and roll, partner, it never gets old."

Caine took another sip of beer, then thought for a moment. "Sounds like a lot of balls to juggle all at once."

"It can be. But once you get the hang of it, it's like riding a bike." Jack finished his beer and slammed the empty bottle on the table. He wiped his mouth with the back of his hand. "Now, how about you tell me what this is all about?"

CHAPTER NINE

TUMACO, COLOMBIA

Tumaco was a shithole, but it was El Lobizon's shithole. He owned this town.

When other men forgot this fact, El Lobizon ensured they never forgot a second time. He jogged their memories with blood and pain.

He didn't understand why anyone would want to move in on his territory anyway. Geographically, Tumaco was unremarkable. It lay in the southwestern most corner of Colombia, near the Ecuadorian border. The peninsula city stretched out over the Pacific Ocean. Overcrowded, hot and oppressively humid, the town was a breeding ground for mosquitos and cockroaches. The drains smelled like sewers, and the sewers smelt worse.

In Tumaco, it rained almost every day. The frequent downpours flooded the gutters with a steady flow of garbage and refuse. The layers of festering debris built up over the decades. The refuse clogged the sewers, making them prone to overflowing. The pools of floating trash swirled beneath thousands of cheap homes, built on stilts covering the muck-clogged waters.

Despite all this, sometimes fools sought to pry the town from El Lobizon's iron grip. He knew it was not the town itself that his enemies craved. It was the business Tumaco supported that was worth taking. El Lobizon controlled the most profitable enterprise in town… the cultivation, manufacture and distribution of cocaine. That was the prize his competitors desired to take from him. But whenever they tried, the legend of El Lobizon was always ready to put them back in their place.

On this particularly muggy, humid day, El Lobizon had arrived early at his warehouse. He needed to count his latest shipments of U.S. dollars, and inventory his supply of cocaine. Luckily for him, the old warehouse he used for such activities was not built over the stinking muck. Instead, it sat on the peninsula proper. Here, the streets were paved, the drains weren't as clogged, and the garbage was removed by municipal services.

Inside, the warehouse wasn't pretty. Fans suspended in the rafters did little more than push the hot, dank air around in circles. Soon El Lobizon felt beads of sweat trickling down his face. He ignored them, and continued counting his money. Sweat was a fact of life he had grudgingly grown to accept.

When he finished counting, El Lobizon wiped his hairy knuckles on his blue cotton pants and sighed. He scratched his fat, even hairier belly. He heard Cuban salsa music playing in another building he owned, a factory next door. He realized the salsa had been playing all morning. He had been so focused on his work he hadn't noticed it before. The music entertained dozens of chica workers… girls who sewed clothes, purses and other goods. Products he sold to the growing number of Americano tourists frequenting Tumaco these days.

But the chicas, the factory and the cheap clothes were all just a front. Another business, through which El Lobizon could launder the drug money he had been counting.

Tuning out the muted salsa, El Lobizon listened instead to the other noises he had ignored all morning. Begging. Moans. Screams…

Earlier, his men had dragged a traitorous underling into a dark, adjacent room. The traitor was stripped and tied to a chair, then beaten. 'Tenderized', as El Lobizon called it.

The cartel leader waited until the cries of pain faded to a quiet whimpering. Then he heaved his bulky frame into a standing position. He scratched his crotch and snorted a wad of black diesel-infused snot from his nostrils. His fingers caressed the gold-plated .357 Magnum revolver in his holster. The mother of pearl grip was decorated with a wolf motif. It matched the gold wolf's head that adorned his belt buckle. He didn't expect to fire the weapon. It was all just part of the show.

Hernando Osorio... that was the name of the captive in the next room. Until yesterday, El Lobizon had considered the man one of his most valued operators. Osorio was responsible for eight cocaine laboratories, spread throughout the mangrove swamps. El Lobizon paused, and thought for a moment. He had to admit, Osorio ran a profitable operation. His facilities were rarely hit by the Colombian Army or DEA paramilitary teams. It would be a shame to lose him. But Osorio had fucked up. Big time.

El Lobizon paced into the dark, dingy room where Osorio was being held. Behind the bruised and sweating man, a dark figure stood in the shadows. He stepped forward into the light. El Lobizon nodded... it was Carlos Supay, his top sicario. Ironically, the cold-blooded killer who had sent so many to the grave was as gaunt and thin as a corpse. His skin had a grey pallor, like that of a dead man. But Supay's frail appearance was deceptive... His body was all lean muscle. El Lobizon knew the killer was as nimble and vicious as a rabid monkey.

Formerly a member of AFEUR, Colombia's Urban Counter-Terrorism Special Forces Group, Supay had jumped sides. Now, he worked for El Lobizon's cartel. But before he was allowed to join the criminal organization, Supay had to prove his loyalty. For his initiation, he brutally murdered all the other members of his AFEUR unit.

Then came their families. Wives, mothers, children… After that, the job was his.

El Lobizon's eyes traveled up and down the man whimpering in the death chair. Blood dripped like a leaky tap from Osorio's nostrils. Supay's knuckles were raw and bloody from the beating he had given the man.

"Jefe!" Osorio pleaded as he wriggled against his bindings. "Please, Jefe. What have I done to offend you?"

El Lobizon circled Osorio. He wanted the man to sweat, to dread whatever fate awaited him.

"El Lobizon? *Por favor…* Please, what have I done?"

El Lobizon placed a hand on Osorio's shoulder. He squeezed until Osorio flinched in pain. "What did I say to you, Osorio? The last time we met."

"What do you mean, Jefe? I'm making money, more this month than ever before. More than all your other operators!"

El Lobizon snorted. "*Si*, this is true. But we could be making more money than that. Much more, if you had listened to me."

Osorio looked up at El Lobizon. He turned to Supay for guidance, but the two men kept their expressions impassive. Osorio had forgotten their last conversation, or was pretending not to have remembered. El Lobizon would make him remember.

"How much of our product do we lose, Osorio? Each time we ship into America?"

Osorio shrugged, confused where this question had come from. "Sixty, maybe seventy percent. But that's not my fault Jefe! We've always known that—"

"And how much do we pay the Mexicans?" El Lobizon continued, cutting the terrified man off. "How much for the so-called privilege of moving our produce over their borders?"

"Five, ten percent?"

El Lobizon growled like a dog, causing the bound man to moan in fear. "I told you, Osorio, the last time we spoke face to face. I told you I had a way to get one-hundred percent of the product into Los Angeles. A way that would keep the filthy Mexicans out of the deal. But you didn't listen. You fucked it up! You shipped the quota I required through our usual supply routes, after I told you not to."

The blood drained from Osorio's face. His eyes grew wide.

El Lobizon smiled. "Now you remember. You piece of shit!"

Tears streamed from Osorio's eyes. Finally, he understood how he had failed his Jefe.

"Did you know?" El Lobizon spoke softly, preparing for the brutal shock to come. "Did you know I am the seventh son of a seventh son?"

"No... I don't—"

It was a lie, of course. A lie he had told countless times. The first of many lies he was about to utter. But the words held power, and that's why they were worth speaking, even to a dead man.

"And did you know that I was never baptized?"

"I had heard Jefe, but it matters not... to me."

El Lobizon pulled off his shirt and hung it on a nail in the wall. He kicked off his shoes and pulled off his socks. Osorio stared wide-eyed, wondering what was transpiring.

"I was born in Buenos Aries," El Lobizon said. "Did you know that?"

He took off his gun and holster, pants and y-fronts, and hung them in turn on the hook. He was as naked as Osorio now. His hairy and fat, yet solid body, now on full display.

"Everyone has heard of me, Osorio. Everyone knows my legend. I am El Lobizon. The Argentinian Werewolf."

"You..." Osorio could barely speak. "You...?"

El Lobizon twisted and tightened all his muscles. He bent over, contorting, as if he were experiencing excruciating pain. "Yes Osorio," he hissed through forced, labored breaths. "I am the monster your *madre* told you about when you were just a *ninito*, a little boy. I am the monster that plagued your nightmares and kept you trembling in bed in the darkest nights."

Supay took his cue and left the room. He had seen El Lobizon's performance many times. He knew what was coming.

As he walked past, Osorio pissed himself. He wept like a girl.

El Lobizon said nothing more.

He stepped into an adjoining room. There was a small work-light clamped to a table within. It sat next to a cage where a Doberman pinscher paced back and forth behind the wire mesh. It was silent, but its eyes emanated a wild, hungry look. The room had been built so that whoever was bound in the chair could not see what was happening in the shadows.

El Lobizon howled like a dog, then rattled the cage again. The dog had been nurtured its whole life on human flesh. His men had tormented it since it was a pup, making it aggressive and volatile. When its movements became twitchy and frantic, El Lobizon knew the beast was ready. Picking up a long sharp stick, he prodded the dog through the bars of the cage until it growled and snarled.

When the animal howled in fury, El Lobizon released the pinscher from his cage. The snarling hound stalked from the shadows into the light of the conference room. Osorio screamed when he laid eyes on the creature. "No El Lobizon!" he pleaded, convinced El Lobizon had become the beast.

The Doberman hadn't eaten in days. It was hungry... Ravenous. The beast sized up the bound man. Recognizing that its prey was defenseless, it bounded across the dirty floor. The ferocious dog leapt straight at the man's throat. Its thick, savage jaws clamped down on Osorio's windpipe.

Blood sprayed everywhere, spattering the walls and floor of the room. Osorio thrashed on his chair for several seconds, until the blood loss became too much. The oxygen levels in his brain slowly faded. A few seconds later, he no longer screamed... He had no throat left to scream with.

In the factory next door, the chicas turned up the salsa music louder. El Lobizon knew they did not wish to hear the things that transpired here in his warehouse. They all knew the stories. If the

Argentinian Werewolf didn't feed each week, it would come for one of them.

As the Doberman pinscher lapped at Osorio's flesh, El Lobizon pulled his shirt back on, and grabbed his pants. There was no need for pretense now... Only Supay was left watching. The howls of the Argentinian Werewolf would have been heard again by his many neighbors. Stories of today's killing would spread through his town, reinforcing his legend.

"We have another problem, Jefe," Supay said. His voice was a low, raspy growl.

"What problem?" El Lobizon snorted as he buckled his .357 wolf Magnum back around his waist. He watched as the dog's pink tongue licked Osorio's lifeless eyeballs.

"The woman," Supay hissed. "The Chinese programmer."

"What about her?"

"She acted as our friend the Captain said she would. She has fled to South America."

El Lobizon nodded. "Of course. Where, exactly?"

Supay grinned, revealing stained yellow teeth. "La Paz."

"Not as close as we thought," El Lobizon said, shrugging.

"No Jefe, but close enough. Should I pay her a visit? Or can she still assist us?"

El Lobizon patted the dog. The beast was compliant now that it had fed. The canine's slobbering mouth was stained with Osorio's blood. He wiped a trail of the crimson liquid on his shirt.

"No," El Lobizon finally answered. "The Captain said her usefulness was at an end. She could be in Bolivia to expose us to her Chinese masters. We should finish this."

Supay grinned. "I can be on a flight to Cali tonight. I will arrive in La Paz tomorrow."

El Lobizon nodded. "Do it."

"Si, Jefe."

"And Supay?"

"Si, Jefe?"

El Lobizon clenched his teeth. His plan to fool the Americans and snub the greedy Mexicans was now in play. But the Chinese programmer was a loose end now. She alone could unravel everything.

"Take four of your best sicarios. Chinese spies may have followed her to Bolivia. They will need to be dealt with, as well as the Americans."

Supay nodded. "Of course Jefe. It will be my pleasure."

Supay left the room. El Lobizon continued stroking his panting dog. He held up his hand. In the room's dim light, he could see strands of crimson liquid, congealing on his skin.

He licked the sticky blood from one of his fingers. It was still warm.

He grinned, and stared into Osorio's dull, lifeless eyes.

"Now you know," he whispered. "Don't you, Osorio? I am the seventh son of a seventh son, and I have not been baptized. I am an abomination in the eyes of our lord. And I cannot die as a man dies. The legend of El Lobizon is eternal."

CHAPTER TEN

LA PAZ, BOLIVIA

After eight days holed up in a safe house, Caine was starting to go a little stir crazy.

In his career with the CIA he'd grown used to waiting. He'd spent hours hiding in run down safe houses in some of the worst corners of the world. Days passing the time until a contact showed, or mission details were finalized. Weeks babysitting double agents, or interrogating enemy captives.

Sometimes the safe houses were in the heart of brutal warzones. Helicopters would buzz overhead, and military patrols marched in the streets. Other times, the hidden locations were far from human settlements, hidden deep in remote wilderness areas. Most, however, were in cities like La Paz. Here, at least, the constant background noise of cars and people reminded Caine he was still connected to other human beings.

Regardless of the location, most of Caine's time in safe houses was spent in boredom. There was nothing to do except eat, sleep, exercise and go over operation plans. He had memorized the details of their current mission until he could recite them in his sleep. Now, there was little he could do to fill the twenty-four hours in a day. Boredom was part of the territory.

Jack Tyler sat in a rickety wood chair peering through a slit in the curtains. He looked as bored as Caine felt. The chair creaked as he shifted his weight back and forth.

As the chair rocked, he kept an eye on the narrow cobbled street outside. This particular safe house was located in the Casco Viejo neighborhood. The historical area was the ancient center of La Paz. The buildings across the street were painted in washed out shades of yellow and green. Their concrete walls were pitted, crumbling and decayed. Wild splatters of graffiti defaced most of the buildings. A few of the older structures featured dark red wooden balustrades, but their wood was weathered and rotting. They too had seen better days.

The people who walked the streets were all Hispanic. They dressed in modern western clothes, but no one wore anything garish or bright. As Tyler watched, clouds darkened the sky and a light rain spattered the streets. The pedestrians hurried their pace, shielding their heads with umbrellas and newspapers.

In the eight days since they had arrived, no one outside had given Caine or Tyler a reason to check them twice.

Tyler glanced over his shoulder at Caine. "When does your girlfriend get here again?"

"She's not my girlfriend," Caine corrected him. He'd been half dozing on a musty lounge chair. He wanted to get some sleep before they were operational, but Tyler seemed eager to talk.

"Yeah bud, whatever." Tyler snorted a laugh. "Don't sweat it. My girlfriend Scarlett Johansson hasn't called me back either."

Caine kept his eyes closed, and exhaled a long, slow breath. "Rebecca will be here."

Tyler grunted, and studied the streets again. He pulled his parka close. Their crumbling villa had no heating system. When night fell, it would get much colder, both inside and out.

Caine knew why Tyler was on edge. The local CIA Station had advised them that three Chinese MSS agents had passed through immigration. They were now operational in La Paz. A CIA surveillance team had tailed the Chinese operatives, but lost them in the city. Caine had no doubt the men were here to keep an eye on Su Liao when she flew in later tonight. There was also a real possibility the MSS agents had been sent to eliminate Caine and Tyler as well. Caine knew the Chinese would do anything to prevent the defection of a valuable asset like Su Liao.

Tyler grabbed a thermos and poured himself another coffee. "We need three people to pull off this op," he finally muttered. "Everything else we need is in place. But it only works with three."

"I know. You did a great job, and everything is good to go. Now we just have to wait."

Tyler looked back to the street. "Freeling said she'd be here three days ago."

"She'll be here."

Caine shifted in the lounge chair. Despite his words, he was restless. Rebecca Freeling was bothering him, and not just because of her unexpected absence.

Since Hong Kong, their relationship had changed. The last time they had spoken was in Baltimore, before she had flown to the United Kingdom. Under normal circumstances, Rebecca would have tried to reach him by now. Caine kept telling himself their lack of contact was due to operational reasons. But his instincts told him it was something else. Something personal.

Did she sense how conflicted his feelings really were? Was she pulling away to protect herself? And if so, wasn't that a good thing?

No wonder Tyler's getting on my nerves, he thought. His partner's doubts mirrored his own... A reminder that not everything was right between him and Rebecca.

"Must be a mind-fuck," Tyler said. "You know, you two being an item. Seeing as she's your boss and all?"

"You ask a lot of personal questions, Jack."

Tyler nodded. "Yeah, I hear you. But this is different. She's on the team. Relationships complicate things for everyone. Me included."

Caine raised an eyebrow. "Speaking from personal experience?"

Tyler grinned and sighed. "Let's just say I made a mistake once, with a woman. Well, not a mistake, but something happened. It changed everything about why I do what I do. Freaked me out, you know? Took a while to get my head out of my ass after that."

Caine was about to ask Tyler to elaborate, but stopped himself. If they got chatty, it would increase the likelihood that he'd talk about Rebecca. There were aspects of their relationship he wasn't ready to reveal. Not to anyone.

"She'll be here," Caine said again. He wished Rebecca would show up so they could stop talking about her.

He stood and joined Tyler at the window to watch the streets. Like Tyler, he kept himself hidden in the shadows to avoid detection.

"You work much in Bolivia?" he asked, changing the subject.

Tyler shook his head. "Little bit, here and there. Mostly I was fighting FARC in Colombia. Drug cartels in Colombia. Training the local military in Colombia. Yeah, Colombia was my stomping ground. Oh, also spent time killing fundamentalist assholes in the Triple Frontier. You know, that shithole where Argentina, Brazil, and Paraguay meet at a bend in the Parana River. Lots of Islamic terrorists down there, oddly enough."

"Why did the Army keep sending you to South America?"

The former Delta Force operator shrugged. "My mother was Chilean. I got my baby blue eyes from my dad, rest his soul. I'm fluent in Spanish and English. Guess some fruit salad-wearing desk jockey thought I was suited for this theatre of operation."

"You serve anywhere else?"

"All the luxury resorts. Iraq. Afghanistan. Libya. Yemen, of course. What about you?"

"Similar places. Nothing I can talk about, sorry."

For a moment Tyler looked offended, but only for a moment.

Special Operations Group was the next level of secrecy up from Delta Force. No one talked about anything.

"You're ex-special forces though, right?" Tyler asked. He looked Caine in the eye. "Don't deny it partner, I know you are. I just can't work out which branch yet."

Caine continued peering out at the street in silence.

"Let me guess. 75th Ranger Regiment?"

Caine ignored him. His attention was drawn to a woman across the street. She stood alone in an alcove, checking messages on her cell phone. Or at least giving the impression that she was. Her clothes were stylish yet unremarkable. Tight jeans highlighted her long slim legs, and practical hiking boots covered her feet. A three-quarter jacket protected her against the cold and rain. Her long hair was dyed jet black, but Caine recognized her at once.

"She's here," Caine said, failing to hide the excitement in his voice. "Rebecca's across the street. She's waiting for us to spot her. She won't want us to clock her as an intruder when she comes to the door."

Caine used the light on his cell phone, and signaled Rebecca with a quick flash. It was enough. She put away her phone and crossed the street, approaching the safe house.

Caine met her at the door. She gave him a light peck on the check. "Everything okay, Tom?" she asked.

"All good. I was starting to worry about you."

She smiled. "Nothing to worry about. Just calling in a few favors. Gathering intel."

Caine knew better than to ask for details. When it came to 'need to know', Rebecca always 'needed to know' more than he ever did.

He showed her upstairs to where Tyler kept surveillance through the window. "Rebecca Freeling. This is Jack Tyler."

Tyler gave a casual salute. "Pleased to meet you, ma'am."

"Likewise. Heard a lot about you, Jack."

He laughed. "It's all true."

Caine watched his two companions. Rebecca was tense, closed

off. Other than that he couldn't read her at all. Tyler appeared to notice her unease as well. He squinted his eyes.

"Something bothering you ma'am?" Tyler asked.

Rebecca bit her lip and looked out at the street. The sun was setting over Mount Illimani, a snow-capped peak that dominated the skyline. "You got the report from the local station house? About the three MSS operatives in town?"

"Yeah, what about them?" Tyler asked.

"I confirmed they're here in the city. But there's more... I picked up a second surveillance team, watching the Chinese."

"Who?" Caine asked, concerned about this sudden change in their circumstances.

Rebecca gave him a grim smile. "I have no idea. But if we want this operation to succeed, we'd better find out."

CHAPTER ELEVEN

Within thirty seconds Caine, Tyler and Rebecca were out on the streets. Each wore a radio with a micro earpiece for communication, and extra layers of clothing to protect against the cold. Caine carried a Sig Sauer P226 handgun. Rebecca pocketed a 9mm Beretta M9 semi-automatic pistol. And Tyler had tucked his favorite Beretta Px4 Storm with .45 ACP rounds into his waistband. The weapons were easy to conceal beneath their thick winter clothing.

"So where are these MSS guys holed up?" Tyler asked, speaking over the radio's throat mic to test it out. His voice crackled over their embedded ear canal receivers.

"In an apartment," Rebecca answered in a low, soft voice. "They're near the El Mercado de las Brujas."

"The Witches Market," Tyler said with a grin. "Of course they are."

They split into two groups. Rebecca and Caine took the lead, holding hands and walking as a couple. Tyler fell behind, but stayed close enough to cover their backs. They crossed a footbridge over the busy Avenida Mariscal Santa Cruz. The curved arch overlooked rows of blue townhouses and decrepit apartment tower blocks. The manicured garden between the express road and the townhouses stuck out like a sore thumb. Much effort had been put into maintaining the colorful flowers and plants. But everything surrounding the manicured strip of land looked decayed and broken.

After taking several narrow streets that twisted through the mountainous city, they entered the Witches Market. Caine, Rebecca and Tyler had no problems blending in. The area was packed with shoppers, including foreign tourists searching for bargains. Pedestrians ambled along the narrow, cobblestone street. They walked past kiosks hawking tours to Machu Picchu and the Amazon rainforest. Other stores promoted cheap but rugged knit clothing. Panama hats and Alpaca woven rugs. Women ran most of the shops. They wore bright colored *Quechan* skirts, and capes with geometric Incan style patterns to attract tourists.

Caine eyed the strange, exotic items for sale in the market. Witch doctors hawked potions made from dried frogs and medicinal plants. Incan sun and moon amulets sparkled next to preserved ocelot skins and dried llama fetuses. Caine had read the latter were often buried under the foundations of Bolivian houses. They were considered a sacred offering to the goddess Pachamama. Bolivia was still a very spiritual country, despite five-hundred years of European influence.

Rebecca led Caine deeper into the market. The sun fell behind the surrounding Andean mountains, leaving the sky cold and black. Street lamps provided some illumination, but they cast inky tendrils of shadow across the market.

"Down there," Rebecca whispered, nodding toward an even darker alleyway. The narrow, twisting passage led away from the main market thoroughfare. "Doesn't look half as inviting at night," she mused.

A Latino man stepped out of the darkness. At first glance, he looked no different to the millions of other men in this country. He wore a smooth black leather jacket and dark, crisp pants. His shoes were expensive and clean. His face was thin and gaunt. Caine wasn't sure what bothered him about the man, but the hairs on the back of his neck tingled.

"Was he here before?" Caine whispered to Rebecca.

She hesitated. "I don't think so."

Caine let the man pass. He spoke into his mic. "Tyler?"

"I see him," Tyler responded. "Sharp dresser. Face like a skeleton Halloween mask?"

"That's the one."

"I'm on him."

"Roger that."

"Look." Rebecca glanced towards the cobblestones in front of them. The gaunt-faced man had left footprints. Caine crouched and touched the dark marking. He felt sticky liquid beneath his fingers. He held it close to his nose and inhaled. The iron tang of fresh blood was unmistakable.

"Blood," Caine whispered.

Rebecca gripped her pistol inside the pocket of her jacket. Caine did the same.

"Tyler?" Caine called on their radio. "Do you have eyes on target?"

"Roger that."

"Get ready to take him out. Wait for my signal."

"Just say the word. He's walking east. Moving at a brisk pace, not looking for a tail. Should be easy."

"Be careful. He's likely armed and dangerous."

"So am I," Tyler replied.

Caine turned to Rebecca. "Which apartment?"

She pointed to the second level of a nearby building, with white-washed walls and wooden windows decorated with potted roses. The wooden door leading inside was half open. No other door on the street was.

"What about Jack?" she asked, her voice tinged with concern.

"He knows what he's doing," Caine whispered. "Stay here and keep watch."

He stepped inside the door. Like most houses in the area, the interior was far nicer and cleaner than the outside. The first floor was furnished with some chairs, side tables and a sofa. Crosses and paintings of Jesus Christ hung from the walls.

The trail of bloody footprints led across the floor. In the dim light, Caine almost tripped over the corpse of a Chinese man. He kneeled down and examined the body. He noted two bullet holes in the corpse's chest. More bloody footprints covered a flight of stairs to his right, moving in both directions.

Caine followed the crimson tracks to the second floor. The stairs creaked under the weight of each step. When he reached the upstairs corridor, he listened for noises as he checked around the corner. Two more bodies lay in the master bedroom. Gaping bullet holes pierced their mangled faces and sopping ribcages. The sheets were a tangled, blood-soaked mess.

A shattered laptop sat on the nightstand next to the bed. Its hard drive had been ripped from its guts.

"Building clear," Caine reported to Rebecca and Tyler. "The second team acted before we got here. Took a hard drive. Killed all three operatives. Execution style."

"I'm only seeing the one target, still walking east," Tyler reported. "He's one cool customer if he took out three MSS agents on his own."

"Nothing happening in the street," Rebecca reported. "When I checked here earlier today there were at least four Latino men watching the apartment. I don't see any of them now."

"That feels wrong," Caine said.

"Why?" Rebecca asked.

"Why would one man come back alone, to kill three highly trained Chinese operatives? When he could have had a hit squad do the job for him?"

Even as the words left his mouth, he knew the answer to his question. Some men worked better alone. Men who were trained to operate alone, who were deadlier operating alone than working with a team. Men who were proficient in killing and subterfuge.

Men like me, he thought.

Caine said nothing more as he descended the creaking steps. He returned downstairs and joined Rebecca on the street. They walked quickly from the Witches Market and headed east. "We're coming for you Tyler. Give us your pos—"

A series of loud cracks echoed from the distant street ahead. Static crackled over the radio.

"Tyler?" Rebecca called anxiously. "Tyler, are you—"

"I've been spotted."

"Are you hit?" Caine hissed.

"No, but he's got me pinned down."

Caine and Rebecca broke into a sprint. "We're headed your way," Caine yelled as his feet pounded the cobblestone. "Give us your exact location."

More gunfire pierced the cold night air. Then the screech of a car's brakes.

"Fuck!" Tyler screamed.

"Tyler, you okay?" Caine asked. "Tyler, answer me!"

The radio was silent. Their footsteps pounded across the cobblestone, echoing off the stone walls around them. Finally, an answer came back through their earpieces.

"I'm good," Tyler grunted. "Close one though. The target has exfiltrated. Van showed up out of nowhere. He got away."

The wail of sirens pierced the night. They were far in the distance, but Caine could hear them moving closer.

"Get out of there," Caine snapped. "Lose the gun."

"Already two hundred steps ahead of you."

Rebecca peeled away from Caine, acting like he didn't exist. "We need to split up," she instructed over the radio. "Plaza Marcelo Quiroga Santa Cruz. We regroup there. I don't need to tell you to watch for tails."

Caine increased his pace, walking away from her at a smooth, consistent speed. He didn't want to act in a way that would alert suspicion. Plaza Marcelo Quiroga Santa Cruz was to the west. It was one of their preplanned rendezvous points, should anything go wrong. And apparently, things had just gone very wrong.

To confuse anyone who might be tailing them, Caine headed south for a few blocks, then west, then north. A convoy of police cars screamed by. Caine looked away, pretending to check messages on his phone. The police cars didn't stop, and soon he was moving again.

Plaza Marcelo Quiroga Santa Cruz was a roundabout lit up by street lights. Taxis, tour vans and four-wheel drives circled the busy street. The center was a park enclosed in a wrought iron fence. Even at this late hour children played with their parents on the lush green field. Along the fence were dozens of stalls selling a variety of clothes. The surrounding buildings were three to five stories high. Caine assumed they were office blocks or apartments.

The three of them met up, then turned and walked downhill along Zolio Flores. A street band in ponchos and sombreros, thinking Caine and Rebecca were tourists, followed after them. They played 'The Lonely Shepard' on their pan flutes. Caine shoved a wad of money at the lead minstrel.

"Sorry. Not in the mood for music," he muttered. The musicians faded back into the shadows. The trio kept walking.

"Jack, what happened?" Rebecca asked. She walked between the two men, but she did not look at either of them as she spoke. All their eyes were darting around the city, scanning the streets and alleys for threats.

"Skeleton Face had an escape plan. Van just showed up, and in he went. The other guys inside spotted me and started shooting. That's about it."

"Did you get a plate number?" Rebecca asked. "Or a description of the men in the van?"

Tyler shook his head. "Negative on both. It was dark, and they were shooting at me. But I have to say, I got a feeling about them."

"What kind of feeling?" asked Rebecca.

"I've seen their kind before. In Colombia, and Mexico. Skeleton Face wasn't afraid, wasn't hiding who he was. Cocky even, like he was invincible. Like no one could touch him."

"Not a special forces or intelligence team then?" Caine asked. Professional state-sponsored paramilitary teams were trained to blend in with their surroundings. They usually went unnoticed, until they made their move. What Tyler described sounded more like an organized crime hit.

"No," Tyler said, and shook his head. "In fact, I'd say they were sicario. A cartel death squad."

"Cartel?" Caine asked. "What the hell would a drug cartel want with a Chinese submarine technician?"

"Got me," Tyler said, keeping his eyes on the dark street ahead of them. "Like I said, it's just a feeling."

Rebecca shook her head. "I can think of a dozen reasons why." She didn't explain further. "Look, we have to focus." She looked at both men, catching their attention. "The op to extract Su Liao... Is everything in place?"

Both men nodded.

Caine looked at Rebecca, trying to read her expression. He knew they were operational and they all had their game faces on, serious and focused. But something didn't sit right with Caine. Rebecca was acting like she didn't trust him.

"Good," Rebecca said. Her voice was low and calm, and she spoke with authority. Whatever was bothering her, Caine knew he and Tyler would follow her orders without question. "Tyler and I will collect the van and get everything ready here. Tom?" She stared into his eyes. He stared back. Rebecca's expression was as cold as the night air.

"Yes Ma'am?"

"Get to Aeropuerto Internacional El Alto. Pick up Su Liao and bring her to the agreed spot."

Caine nodded. "Will do."

A cold wind blew across the cobblestone street. Rebecca brushed a strand of long dark hair out of her face. "Good," she replied. "Then there's only one thing left to do after that... We kill her."

CHAPTER TWELVE

AEROPUERTO INTERNACIONAL EL ALTO, BOLIVIA

Su Liao's heart raced. She felt dizzy, and her mouth was dry. When she tried to speak, her voice cracked.

Despite her panicked state, she knew exactly what was causing these symptoms. She was terrified beyond belief.

Ever since boarding the flight to South America, every waking moment she felt like she would die. She was certain her terror and anxiety would strangle her heart, and stop it from beating. That fear itself would kill her. But it didn't.

She passed through customs without incident. As she made her way through the baggage claims, her brown eyes darted around the airport. She glanced at the crowd of tourists, keeping an eye out for anyone who might be looking for her. But no one seemed to pay her any mind.

Taking a deep breath, she slung her pack over her shoulder and entered the public terminal. She darted through the crowd, pushing her way past shops and cafes. People were everywhere. Men approached her, jabbering about taxis and hotels. Others waved cardboard signs with names written in black marker. Su noticed she was the only Asian person in the terminal. Most of the crowd consisted of Caucasian and African-American tourists.

She readjusted her backpack and kept moving. Bolivia's main airport followed the same design of every other airport she had visited in Asia. Modern air bridges and steel girder roofs arched overhead. Baggage trolleys and security carts zoomed past her. Hanging signs indicated terminal numbers, ATM's and toilets. Only billboards were different. They advertised local activities for tourists.

As she walked past a towering sign featuring a jaguar stalking through the jungle, she realized she was being followed. Two men were walking on either side of her, matching her pace. Before she could move away, they closed in and bumped her. The man on her left grabbed her arm. She felt something cold and sharp press against her kidney. Su gasped, and froze in place. A single twist of the man's wrist and the blade would impale her.

The other bearded man took her backpack and slung it over his shoulders. "*Senorita*," the man with the knife hissed. He had a reedy, whistling voice. "Bolivia can be a dangerous country for young, pretty women like yourself."

A tremor ran across her face, but she said nothing. She tried to control her shaking. She realized her fear had been justified. After coming so far, after finally escaping China... She was about to be murdered before she could even leave the airport.

Together they approached a men's room. A plastic sign on the floor blocked the doorway, indicating the toilet needed maintenance. The men kicked the sign aside, and led her inside. She coughed, then gagged. The dingy room stank of urine, and a pool of dirty water sloshed across the floor. The open stalls reeked of fecal matter, and overflowed with used paper towels.

Two men stood waiting inside. Each held a semi-automatic pistol with silencers. They wore identical maintenance uniforms, but Su knew they weren't cleaners.

The man with the knife spun her around and pressed his chest up against her back. He looped an arm around her neck. With his free hand, he pressed the knife into her soft throat. He spun her around and pushed her forward, towards the mirror hanging above the wash basins. Su could see his reflection in the spattered, cracked glass.

Despite his wiry frame and gaunt features, he was incredibly strong. She knew she would not be able to break his hold on her. She was too terrified to even try.

"He said you would run," the skeletal man hissed. "I'm so glad. I'm going to enjoy working on you." He lowered the knife to her sweater and sliced through the wool. He continued making long, slow cuts. He dragged the blade along her clothes, until the sweater and most of her shirt underneath hung in tatters.

A tremor ran through Su's body. Tears streamed down her face, and a barely audible whimper escaped her lips. "Please," she whispered in English. "Please, I swear I won't—"

"Shhhhhh!" The gaunt man pressed the cold knife to her lips. "Soon you will see. This blade goes through flesh just as easily." He grinned when he saw the look of terror in her eyes. One of the men behind them chuckled. She would have fainted if the skeletal man's grip wasn't tight around her.

He cut again. The remains of her sweater fell to the floor.

Su froze in fear. She'd read how drug cartels tortured their victims. Slit their throats and pulled their tongues out through the butchered windpipe. 'Colombian neckties', they call it.

"Wha... What do you want?" she asked, still speaking English. She did not speak Spanish, and it seemed unlikely these men could understand Chinese. "Did Zhao Jianyu send you?"

The skeletal man grinned like a harlequin clown. The effect of his smile was even more unsettling. "Oh, *Senorita*, you don't know the half of it." He sliced away what little remained of her shirt, until she stood wearing only her bra. She knew he would cut that away soon, then her pants. Then a long, slow butchering of her flesh...

Her attacker paused and turned to his bearded underling, then barked orders in Spanish.

The bearded man stepped up to the sink. Glancing up at the mirror, Su could see he wore a thick gold necklace, and his hair was slicked back with gel. He emptied the contents of her pack into the sink. Some loose tees and panties fell out, followed by half a bottle of water, some toiletries and a local guidebook. He picked out a pair of her panties and sniffed them.

"Please," she whimpered again. Please don't kill me."

The leader's knife was back at her throat. "Oh, do not fret. We won't kill you... Not yet." His grin grew wider. "First we're going to have some fun."

The knife tickled her throat. A tiny droplet of blood fell from her skin, and splashed in the sink.

Suddenly, the bathroom door flew open. It crashed into the wall, and the sound echoed through the small, dank room like a canon.

A man charged inside.

Su could barely see what was happening in the filthy, chipped mirror. She heard men scuffling, saw a few quick flashes of motion in the streaked glass. One of the men in the cleaner's uniform hit the ground with a loud thud.

The bearded man's silenced pistol made a coughing sound as it fired. But the intruder already had the other cleaner in a hold, and used the body as a human shield. A pattern of crimson dots spread across the man's uniform. Ducking down, the intruder released the corpse and raised a gun of his own.

More shots whined through the bathroom. The bearded man's head snapped back. Blood and brain fragments spattered the white sinks. A stray shot hit the mirror and it exploded into a thousand shimmering fragments.

The skeletal man dropped Su. She fell to the urine-soaked floors, screaming and crying. She covered her head with her hands and curled into a fetal position.

The leader charged toward the intruder, his knife slashing a wide arc through the air. The intruder tried to spin around and target the gaunt man, but he was too close... a crimson gash sliced across the intruder's shooting arm. Blood stained the sleeve of his jacket, and his pistol clattered to the floor.

The tall, gangly man shoved past him, and fled the men's room. He did not spare even a second to look back at his fallen comrades. One moment he was there. The next, he was gone.

The intruder stood still for a moment, panting for breath. Then he walked over to Su and offered his hand. He helped her up off the stinking floor. She was still trembling, shivering uncontrollably. He removed his jacket and gently draped it around her shoulders.

Su was still dizzy from fear and shock, and her vision was blurred. But she instantly recognized the man's warm smile and piercing, emerald green eyes. She threw her arms around him, and pressed her face into his chest.

Thomas Caine had just saved her life.

CHAPTER THIRTEEN

"We've got to get out of here," Caine said as he recovered his pistol and slid it into the waistband of his jeans. "Are you hurt?"

Su Liao shook her head. "No... No." She gave a nervous laugh. "I can't seem to stop shaking, but I'm okay."

Caine removed his thick wool sweater. He tore the sleeves from his shirt, and used the materials as a makeshift bandage. Working quickly, he wrapped the fabric around the long, crimson gash along his forearm. He tied off the bandage, then pulled the jumper back on and washed his hands.

His jacket hung loose on her slim body, but Su slipped her arms in the sleeves and zipped up the front. She then wrapped her arms across her chest and rubbed her shoulders. "Who were those men?"

"Colombian cartel. Hitmen." Caine took her arm and led her outside. His eyes swept across the terminal, scanning the area for threats. The sicarios' gaunt leader was long gone. No one else seemed to have noticed the commotion that had transpired. The airport was noisy and the PA system broadcast frequent announcements. He was confident no one would have heard the silenced gunfire through the closed door.

"Keep moving," Caine ordered.

It was dark when they stepped outside the airport. Su checked her watch. The local time was just after midnight, but jet lag made her feel like it was the middle of the afternoon. They crossed over to the short-term car park. Caine took her to a Mazda 3 sedan and unlocked the doors with the key fob remote. "Get in."

Su slipped into the passenger seat. Her face was pale, and she covered her mouth with her hands. Suddenly, she was gagging. She opened the door and vomited her breakfast onto the pavement. She coughed and retched again, as another spasm ran through her stomach. Then she sat back in her seat and closed her eyes.

"I'm sorry," she said. "I just—"

"Don't worry about it," Caine replied. "It's normal. Just breathe."

He reached over and closed her door. Then he accelerated through the car park, stopping to pay with cash at the exit gate. Then they sped off, heading west away from La Paz. Streetlights and traffic were the only pinpoints of illumination in the dark streets.

Caine dialed a number on his cell phone. "I have the asset," he said after the call connected. "We proceed with the plan, Highway Nineteen, on the overpass at Avenue Bolivia. There was an incident at the airport, but the original extraction point still stands."

He ended the call and slipped the phone into his pocket. He turned to Su. "There are new clothes in the back. Get changed."

Su nodded. She turned around, and grabbed the bag sitting on the back seat. "What happens now?" she asked.

"We have a plan. But for it to work, you need to look the part."

Su said nothing as she slipped into the new clothes. The outfit appeared to be rugged hiking gear... jeans, boots, a wool sweater knitted with a geometric Incan pattern, and a rain jacket. As they sped along the dark road, she was grateful no one could see inside the car. She shimmied into the jeans, then began tying the laces of the boots.

"You still have your passport?" Caine asked.

She nodded.

"Hang onto that. Everything else has to go." Caine took her pile of old clothes and threw them out the window as they drove. Su was too stunned to ask why.

After that, Caine drove in silence. His eyes kept glancing from the windshield to the rearview mirror. Su realized he was watching the roads, both ahead and behind them. Sometimes he would even turn and monitor the sky out the driver's side window, even though thick, dark clouds blocked out the stars.

"What are you looking for?" Su asked, still tasting the bile in her mouth.

"We're being followed," Caine explained. "A Mitsubishi Outlander with four men inside. Right now they're three cars behind us. One of them is the man with the knife, from the bathroom. The one who got away."

"How do you know that? It's pitch black outside."

Caine grinned. "They stopped next to us at traffic lights a few kilometers back. The light from stores lit up the interior for a few seconds. They were easy enough to spot."

Su shuddered. She was almost sick again. "What... What do they want with me?"

Caine grinned again, but narrowed his eyes. "I think you know the answer to that better than I do."

Su's lips parted, but she said nothing. He looked into her eyes for a second, then turned his piercing gaze back to the road. She continued to stare at him, like a deer frozen in headlights. Finally, she nodded, and took a deep breath. "You are right, Mr. Caine. The matter is far more complicated than I let on in Macau."

"It usually is."

"When I said my life was in danger, I was not lying. There is a submarine captain... He coerced me into falsifying his navigation records. He is using his current mission as cover to hide his criminal activities from the MSS, and others in the Chinese government."

Caine raised an eyebrow. Su noticed again that Caine was a handsome man. His strong chiseled jaw and thick, dark brown hair were attractive enough. But his eyes... It was his deep, soulful eyes, green as jade stones, that impressed her the most. He had an aura about him. If not for him, the men in the bathroom... She shuddered, banishing those thoughts from her mind. But she also had seen first hand that Caine could be a cool and efficient killer when the situation warranted it. He seemed to want to protect her... But for how long? What if she became a liability?

"Do you know who Captain Zhao Jianyu is?" she finally asked.

"PLA Navy submarine captain. Well connected with the Chinese Communist Party."

Su nodded. She squeezed her hands tight in frustration and fear. "Some time ago, he used his connections to have my parents arrested and imprisoned. He told me if I didn't falsify navigation records for his mission, he would ensure they were killed."

Caine glared at her. More streetlights rushed by outside. "What exactly is this mission of his?"

"His official objective is to get his submarine as close to the west coast of the United States as possible, without being tracked. The PLA Navy wants to test the stealth capabilities of our new submarine fleet."

"What's he running?" Caine asked.

"Type 093. It's called the *Hai Long*. The name means 'Sea Dragon'."

"Type 093?" Caine shot her a glance as they sped around a tight bend. "I didn't think they existed yet?"

"They exist. You Americans aren't supposed to know about them yet. The PLA Navy wants to assess their capabilities. Especially when combined with cyber-attacks on your NRO spy satellites."

Caine nodded. "To pull this off, Zhao would have to take his sub well south of the Hawaiian ops areas. He'd have to head west of Kauai and south of Oahu to avoid detection."

"That's right," Su answered, her voice quivering. "Hawaii was factored in."

"So that's what the PLA Navy thinks he's doing... what's his real objective?" Caine asked.

Su turned and looked out the window. Caine could see her reflection in the glass. Her eyes were dark and wide as she gazed into the blackness outside the car.

"Su..." he said in a low voice.

She spun around and faced him. "If I tell you, you have to promise you will get me safely to America. You must protect me!"

Caine tightened his grip on the wheel. "I'll do my best. But until I know what's really going on, I can't promise anything."

Su watched Caine for a moment. She took another deep breath. "Why do you think Colombian drug cartels and a Chinese submarine crew would work together? It could only be for one purpose. A Type 093 has six torpedo tubes. Each torpedo weighs approximately sixteen-hundred kilograms."

"Of course," Caine growled. "Cocaine. Nine thousand, six hundred kilograms of pure cocaine, smuggled into America on a submarine that no one can detect."

Su nodded, her expression grim.

Caine did some mental math, then shook his head. "At a street value of one hundred and fifty dollars per gram, we're talking, what? One and a half billion dollars in a single shipment?" He whistled. "So what's Zhao's cut?"

"I don't know, but it will be substantial," Su replied in a meek voice. "If Zhao succeeds, he will become incredibly wealthy. With that kind of money and power, he will rise far in the Communist Party."

"Does he have the cocaine onboard already?"

She hesitated for a moment. "I believe so," she said.

"So, his special delivery on the way." He gazed out the window, then turned to her. "We'll get word to Langley. They can pass the information onto the Navy, the Coast Guard and the DEA."

"Drug Enforcement Administration?" she asked.

Caine nodded and looked again in the rearview mirror.

"Are we still being followed?" she asked.

"We are. They think they haven't been noticed. They want to see where we go."

"What are we going to do?"

Caine grinned. "We stick to the plan."

"I thought your plan was to fool the Ministry of State Security? But they aren't even here."

"We don't know that. Besides, what works for the MSS will work for the cartel as well. So we stick to the plan." He turned and offered her a smile. "Got it?"

She nodded. Her lip quivered, but she forced herself to return his confident grin. "Got it."

They drove on. Despite the cold outside, Su rolled down her window. La Paz was surrounded by the mountains of the Altiplano range. The altitude in the city was well over three and a half thousand meters. She felt starved for oxygen. The air outside was cool and thin.

She watched as they drove. The vehicle cruised at sixty, maybe seventy kilometers per hour. As they drove through a quaint mountain town, Su saw garden beds protected by bright yellow curbs. Buildings were brick or concrete slabs, covered in graffiti. Like military bunkers, the ground floors were protected by roller shutters or caged doors. Dark windows hid behind thick curtains or mirrored glass. Few people walked the streets in the cool night air.

Bolivia was nothing like China.

"What about your parents?" Caine asked after some time. Su had almost dozed off, and his question startled her. "Now that you have defected, won't their lives be in danger?"

"There is nothing I can do for them," she murmured, choking on her words. "I'm almost certain they have been executed already. And with my usefulness at an end, it would be easier for Zhao Jianyu if they disappeared forever."

Caine stared back at her as more streetlights blazed overhead. Finally, he turned back to the road. He said nothing.

She decided to ask the question that had been plaguing her mind for the longest time. "Mr. Caine, what's going to happen to me?"

"We fake your death. We smuggle you into Peru. Then we fly you to the United States. From there, you show us how to hack into your submarine navigation program. You'll work for us."

"And when you have everything you need from me, what then?"

Caine sighed. "Look, the U.S. isn't perfect, but we have rules, and laws. You'll be safe there, Su Liao. That I can promise."

She wasn't sure she believed him. But she had to remind herself that China had very different values. China was about tradition, control, honor... control. How was it even possible to compare the two countries, when they were fundamentally different on so many levels?

Caine slowed to a halt, and parked the car near a bridge that crossed over another slow-moving highway. "Okay. Here we go," he said. All traces of humor and emotion had left his voice. "Listen very carefully. Do everything I say, when I say it. There's no margin for error here."

She bit her lip. "I will do my best," she said quietly.

Caine stared back at her, his emerald eyes blazing in the dim glow of the streetlights. "I know you will. I don't mean to scare you, but we have to stick to the plan. Otherwise, your death won't be fake after all. Understand?"

She nodded silently.

Caine opened the car door and stepped out into the chilly night air. "Good. Then let's get this done."

CHAPTER FOURTEEN

Caine handed Su a tiny radio earpiece and told her to slip it into her ear canal. He glanced at the car that was tailing them. It had pulled over into the brush across the street.

Su glanced in the rearview mirror as she inserted the tiny earpiece. Four men got out of the other car. She could see them moving beneath the street lights. They all held pistols. They walked at a brisk pace, stalking towards them across the pavement.

"Su, listen to me," Caine said in a firm but quiet voice. "No matter what happens, you are going to run towards that bridge. When we give the signal, you jump."

"What? Into the traffic?"

"Don't argue. You'll be safe. But your jump has to be timed precisely. Another man will give you the signal. Jack, you listening?"

"Copy that," came the voice of another American over the radio. "We're moving into position. T minus one minute."

Caine drew his pistol and pointed it at Su's head. She gasped.

"What are you—"

"We need to make this look like I'm trying to kill you," Caine snapped. "Get out of the car now. Run to the bridge. I'm going to start firing. It might get close, but I promise I won't hit you. Now go!"

Confused and terrified, Su stumbled from the car. She staggered as her feet struck the shoulder of the road. She almost fell as she ran towards the bridge.

She heard shooting. Two cars skidded to a halt in the street, nearly crashing into each other. She heard bullets, thudding into the ground near her feet. She glanced back for a moment. Caine fired one last shot in her direction. Then he pivoted and sent a burst of gunfire towards the advancing men. The surprised kill team ducked low and scrambled for cover. Caine had them pinned down.

Su raced to the bridge. The sound of the gunshots sent her heart racing once again. She was terrified she might not be able to do what was asked of her. But then she remembered the leering smile of the skeleton-faced man in the bathroom… the cold kiss of his knife, as he slid the blade across her skin. She decided she would rather be crushed under the wheels of a car than die at the hands of a man like that.

A voice crackled over her earpiece. "Doing great, Su," said the second American. "We're almost there. You need to be ready to jump in ten seconds."

Su couldn't speak. She heard more gunshots roaring in the darkness behind her. She saw terrified passengers, glancing at her from cars as they sped past. She felt numb, barely aware of her surroundings. She was moving on instinct and adrenaline now. She climbed up on the concrete lip of the bridge. Beneath her, the headlights of the cars rushed through the roundabout. The pavement lay ten or twelve meters below her.

"Okay Su, almost there," came the American. "On my mark, you need to jump. Five…"

Su felt the wind blowing around her. Her legs quivered like jelly.

"Four…"

She felt her foot slip against the concrete. She gasped as she struggled to recover her balance.

"Three..."

More gunshots exploded in the distance. She looked back, but the men were too far away... She could see nothing in the velvety-black darkness. If Caine failed, the vicious killers would come after her again...

"Two..."

What have I gotten myself into? she wondered. What if it was too late, and her life was destroyed anyway?

"Su, jump!" the American shouted. "Jump now!"

The shouted order cut through the rising tide of panic that filled her mind. It was all the incentive Su needed.

She blinked. Then she jumped.

She was falling. She closed her eyes as the wind rushed around her.

She felt a sudden, soft impact. She opened her eyes. She had hit a tarpaulin, then mattresses beneath that.

Su was in the back of a truck, sprawled on her back. She looked up in time to see a muscular man lift the corpse of a young woman. Su realized the dead body was wearing the same clothes she was. The man heaved the corpse out the back of the truck as they drove beneath the underpass.

"All clear," the man said over his radio earpiece. He rolled down the back door as the truck picked up speed. He leaned over to Su and offered a hand, helping her sit up on the tarp. "Nice landing, Miss Laio."

She was still trembling. "Who... who was...?"

"Who was that I threw out the back? Don't sweat it. Former resident of the local morgue," he said, grinning. "Young Asian tourist who wasn't as lucky as you. She died a few weeks ago, after a climbing accident." He shook her hand enthusiastically. "Name's Jack Tyler, by the way."

"Thank you," she mumbled. She could barely collect her thoughts as they sped away into the night. Caine had been true to his word. They had faked her death. "Wait, what about Mr.

Caine?" she asked, suddenly worried for his wellbeing now she was safe.

"Tom's a big boy. He can take care of himself."

"Caine's extracted himself from the shootout," a third voice said over her earpiece. Another American, but this one was a woman. "He'll meet us at the rendezvous in two hours," she said.

"Hear that?" Tyler said with another grin. "Everything's going to plan."

Suddenly Su was gagging again. Her fear had finally caught up with her. But this time, she could only dry heave. There was nothing left in her stomach to cough up.

CHAPTER FIFTEEN

VIACHA, BOLIVIA

As dawn light crawled across Bolivia, Caine sat waiting in his Mazda. He was parked on a dirt road next to a cement factory on the outskirts of Viacha, a large town west of La Paz. Grey clouds gathered in the skies. The thin morning air was crisp and dry.

Soon enough, Tyler's truck pulled onto the tiny road. He parked inside the crumbling plant, keeping the vehicle out of sight from casual observation. Rebecca, Tyler and Su Liao transferred to the Mazda. Caine hit the accelerator as soon as their doors slammed shut. They headed west. He was tired. He hadn't slept in twenty-four hours. But that wasn't going to stop him from getting them all out of the country in one piece.

"Any problems?" Caine asked, as the factory disappeared in the dust behind them.

Tyler leaned back in the passenger seat and closed his eyes. "That's a negative."

Caine glanced back at Rebecca and Su through the rear vision mirror. Rebecca looked as tired as he felt, but Su was an anxious bundle of nerves. Under the circumstances, Caine couldn't blame her.

"What happens now?" she asked.

"We get to the border," Rebecca explained. Her hands massaged her temples. "It's only an hour away. We have a passport for you, Su. A United States passport. You and I cross together, Caine and Tyler will go separately. On the other side we drive to Arequipa. Then we get on a plane and fly to Miami."

"That simple?" Su asked.

Rebecca nodded. "That simple."

Caine kept a watchful eye on the rearview mirror as he drove, but there was no sign they were being followed. They crossed the border into Peru without incident. It was late afternoon when they made their first stop at a gas station. Arequipa was still a few hours away, but it was time for a break. Caine was dead tired, and needed to sleep on the next leg of the journey. Tyler filled the tank, while they all stretched their legs.

Rebecca kept an eye on Su while they used the bathroom together. Not that they were expecting Su to run, but they couldn't rule out the possibility altogether. When Su got back in the car, Rebecca joined Caine. He was leaning against the vehicle's hood, watching people. Together, they observed a group of wrinkled Quechan women in their colorful skirts, ponchos and Panama hats drinking coca leaf tea.

The old women laughed and joked. They were happy souls despite their subsistence lifestyles. In the Andes coca tea was drunk everywhere, and it was legal. As a tea it was harmless, no different to Darjeeling or Earl Grey. Caine had heard coca tea helped with altitude sickness, but he had no need to try it himself. His constitution had not been affected by their elevation.

"I can hear the gears turning in your head," Rebecca said, adding a chuckle. She leaned next to him, and nudged him with her arm.

Caine offered her a tired smile. He wanted to tell her the truth, tell her he was contemplating their future. But he couldn't bring himself to talk about their relationship right now. He was afraid of what might come out. Instead, he replied, "I'm thinking about Su."

"You have a read on her yet?" Rebecca asked. The cool breeze blew a strand of hair across her face. Caine saw that her fiery red hair was starting to show now that the dye was fading. She looked good with dark hair, but he preferred her natural color.

"She's scared," he said. "She's starting to realize, there's no going back now. She feels guilty about abandoning her parents, even though she knows they are likely dead by now." Caine exhaled, and stared down the long, empty road ahead of them. "She's probably wondering if she can trust us too."

Rebecca crossed her arms and shivered. "Understandable. I hope she was worth the effort."

Caine glanced back at her. "You're still not convinced? You think she could be a double agent?"

"I think Jezebel Yan is a smart woman. I trust her instincts."

Caine thought back to their time in Hong Kong. Rebecca had come to life operating in the Far East. Her career was going somewhere there, but Macau had ruined all of that. Now she was playing babysitter to a defector who might have nothing to offer.

If Su Liao didn't produce actionable intelligence, then all their careers with the CIA would take a huge step backwards. Caine didn't care so much. He was used to being sent from one hell hole to the next, always getting the job done. He lived his life one mission at a time. But Rebecca wasn't like that. She had a plan and she knew what she had to do to make that plan a reality. It wouldn't surprise Caine if she had her eye on the Deputy Director of the Clandestine Service. Her career was everything to her.

How could he force her to jeopardize that, when he knew he was going to have to leave her?

He rubbed his tired eyes. A flicker of motion drew his attention. Su Liao exited the car, hugging her body against the cold winds. She marched to Rebecca and Caine. Her expression was sour. "There is something I haven't told you."

"And what would that be?" Rebecca asked carefully.

"Before I hand over access codes to PLAN's submarine navigation systems, you must do one more thing for me."

"Go on?" There was an edge of annoyance in Rebecca's tone. Caine knew she didn't like surprises or people playing games with her. Even though this was the CIA, where every day was a game of deceit, half-truths and straight out lies.

"Zhao Jianyu," Su said forcefully. "I know where he's going to be... the day after tomorrow."

Caine, surprised by this revelation, raised an eyebrow. "Su, I thought you said he already had the cocaine. If that's true, Zhao won't surface until he reaches U.S. waters."

Su shook her head. "I lied then. Now I am not lying."

"If you have something to say, now's the time," Rebecca snapped. "We've already reported to Langley. We told them what you told us, about the *Hai Long*, attempting to bring cocaine into America."

Su Liao shook her head. "That's all true, but there's more. I know exactly where Zhao will be. Remember, he forced me to fake the *Hai Long's* routes across the Pacific, to match the navigation logs when they are checked later. It was Zhao who had my parents arrested. It was Zhao who..." —she paused, as her eyes teared up— "He ordered their deaths."

No one said a word. This, at least, they knew was most likely true.

Su continued. "Zhao doesn't have the drugs yet. I faked his travel plans, but to do so I had to know his real route, in order to change the coordinates. I know when he will pick up the shipment of drugs, in the waters off Tumaco, Colombia."

"Why are you telling us this now?" Caine asked.

She looked away, bit her lip and shifted her weight from one leg to the other. She was clearly nervous and scared. "If you want me to help you, I need you to kill him. I will never be safe while Zhao is alive."

"That's impossible," Rebecca countered. "If we attack Zhao, the Chinese will know that their nav system is compromised. They'll close the backdoor, and we'll lose any chance on gaining real intelligence on PLAN's operations."

"It's worse than that," Caine added. "A direct attack on a Chinese submarine will be interpreted as an act of war."

Su shook her head in disbelief. "You would let ten tons of pure cocaine into your country without lifting a finger to stop it? That's an act of war in itself."

"We have to think of the greater good here, Su!" Rebecca said, raising her voice in anger. "What did you think we'd do? Drop some depth charges and be done with it?"

"I don't care about the drugs," Su cried. "I don't care about the submarine! Just kill Zhao. You must! If you cannot, then send me back to China. I'd rather face a quick death there than spend the rest of my life living in fear. Wondering each day when Zhao's assassins will find me."

Rebecca sighed. She made no attempt to mask her frustration. "You will be safe in America, Su. I promise. No one will touch you there. You'll have a new identity. A new life. Everything."

Su stared back at her. Her eyes were cold and determined. "Do this, or I won't give you the codes."

"Su!" Rebecca exclaimed through gritted teeth. "We'll send word to the Drug Enforcement Administration. They'll intercept the cocaine after it has been offloaded and brought into America."

"But Zhao will still be alive. And rich! With all that money, nothing will stop him from coming after me."

Caine squinted at the girl. Something was off... He couldn't put his finger on it, but he sensed there was still more Su Liao wasn't telling them. But one thing was clear... the girl was scared. Really scared. But about what exactly, he wasn't sure.

"There may be a way," Caine said.

"Tom, are you crazy?" Rebecca snapped, turning her angry glare towards him.

"We don't need to attack the submarine," he continued. "Just the cocaine. If we can destroy it before it gets to Zhao, he won't get paid..."

Rebecca considered his plan for a moment. Then her mouth formed a reluctant smile. "That could work. But it would have to be completely off the books. You'd have to make it look like a rival cartel hit."

Caine nodded. "Tyler's operated in Colombia for years. He and I could fly up there in time for the delivery. Destroy the shipment before it even reaches the submarine."

"What about Zhao?" Su demanded, almost in tears now. "You have to promise me this!"

"That ship has sailed, Su," Rebecca said firmly. "But think about it. This is a good plan. To pull off something like this, Zhao must have promised payoffs to a lot of dangerous people. When it fails, he won't be able to make good on those promises. He'll have so many enemies coming after him, he won't have time to worry about you."

Su looked ready to argue, but her determination seemed to drain from her features. She looked down and sighed.

"What do you say, Su?" Rebecca was firm. "You want to tell us where and when this is going down? Because if you want to take down Zhao... this is the best shot you're ever going to get."

CHAPTER SIXTEEN

TUMACO, COLOMBIA

Jack Tyler expertly handled the Cessna 172 Skyhawk on its final decent into La Florida Airport. The tiny airport grew larger by the second beyond the cockpit windows. The vast, blue ocean ran along one side of the narrow landing strip, and dense mangrove forests surrounded the area. A single bridge connected the airport to the main peninsula city of Tumaco and the rest of Colombia.

Beyond the mangroves to the south, lush jungles carpeted the landscape. Winding rivers and their tributaries cut through the verdant land like veins. Caine considered the water depth. Would it be possible to pilot a submarine up one of the twisting, reed-choked rivers? He doubted it, but he couldn't say for sure.

"Lieutenant Julia Valencia is my contact in Colombia," Tyler explained. He banked the small plane left as they prepared for their final approach. "Sweet lady. She's with DIRAN, *Direccion de Antinarcoticos*, a.k.a. Colombia's Anti-Narcotics Directorate. Based in Cali."

"She drove all this way, to meet you?"

Tyler nodded. "Like I said... Sweet lady."

"Is she on anyone's payroll?" Caine asked in a matter of fact tone. In his experience, corruption in Latin America was as common as coca leaves. It wouldn't have surprised Caine if Tyler had said yes.

If Tyler took offense to the question, he didn't show it. "No way," he said, and chuckled. "Julia's as dependable as they come. When I explained what we were up to, she couldn't resist. A bust this big will make her career."

"Did you tell her it was a Chinese submarine shipping the drugs?"

Tyler grinned. "Not a chance. She'd think I was loco if I let that slip."

"You trust her?"

Tyler nodded. "Julia saved my life once, after an operation in Bogota went south."

"Do I want to know?"

Tyler grinned, lowering the flaps on the Cessna to slow their final approach. "Probably not."

Caine reflected on the last couple of days. The Cessna was a former drug smuggling plane impounded in Peru. Tyler obtained it by making a few quick calls to the local DEA office in the capital, Lima. After clearing things with the Peruvian Anti-Narcotics Agency, they secured the plane and registered a flight-path. Luckily, the aircraft was fitted with long-range fuel tanks, a remnant of its drug running days.

After ensuring Rebecca Freeling and Su Liao were safely on their flight to Miami, Caine and Tyler had taken their own path. It was a two and a half thousand mile journey from Arequipa to Tumaco. They flew low over the harsh deserts, then between the snow-capped peaks of the Peruvian Andes. Next they sped along the vast stretches of the western Amazon rainforest, and across the Ecuadorian Andes. The views had been spectacular, and the scale of the Andean range and the Amazonian rainforest had impressed Caine.

Tyler knew where all the secret airfields were from his former assignments. They touched down on obscure runways in the Amazon jungle, where he negotiated refueling and some hearty meals in exchange for U.S. dollars. They'd spent the previous night in an Indian village on Peru's Maranon River, a tributary of the Amazon itself. They slept under mosquito nets in a bungalow with thousands of bugs crawling on the ceiling. The owner's pet, a python named Alberto, curled up on the floor under Caine's bed. The old man who owned the bungalow told them it would keep the rats away while they slept.

True to the leathery old man's word, no rodents disturbed their slumber.

Now they were finally in Tumaco, Columbia. The airport was coming up fast and soon the wheels touched the old bitumen runway.

As they taxied towards the airport's terminal, Caine mentally prepared himself for what lay ahead. News of two westerners flying in unannounced on a former drug plane would spread fast. The wrong kind of people would take notice. Caine and Tyler had to be out of the airport and in a safe house as fast as possible.

After they parked their plane, they stepped out into the hot, muggy air. Caine felt under prepared. They were armed with nothing more than side-arms and knives. That didn't seem enough for what they were about to do. But Tyler seemed confident Lieutenant Valencia would provide them all the equipment they needed.

"There she is," Tyler said as a slim woman in her early thirties approached through the heat-rippled air. She wore skin-tight cargo pants and a crisp t-shirt. Like most Latin American women, she had dark hair and coffee-colored skin. She smiled and waved at Tyler. He waved back, but Caine squinted at the woman as she walked closer. Her movements seemed stiff, unnatural somehow.

"I don't like this," Caine muttered to Tyler.

"Would you relax? I trust Julia with my life. Not many people I can say that about."

The hairs on the back of Caine's neck tingled. His instincts sent jolts of adrenaline through his nerves. His hand hovered towards his waistband. He trusted Tyler's judgment, but he knew something wasn't right. "Are you sure?" he muttered.

The smiling Julia Valencia was within ten meters of them when she froze in place. "Tyler," she shouted. "You crazy *perro* son of a bitch—" As she spoke her hand darted behind her back and drew a pistol.

She moved fast, but Caine was faster. Before Valencia could aim her weapon, Caine's SIG Sauer was in his hands and trained on the woman.

She continued swinging the pistol up, drawing a bead on Tyler.

Without conscious thought, Caine squeezed the trigger. The muzzle exploded with fire and noise as he put a bullet through her thigh. She fell to the tarmac, gasping in pain.

Caine sprinted over to her. With a swift kick, he sent her Jericho 941 semi-automatic clattering across the runway. He aimed his pistol at her head.

Tyler came up behind, his Beretta Px4 Storm at the ready. "What's going on?" he said, his question directed as much at Caine as at Valencia. He looked down at the woman, his face filled with shock and anger. "Julia, why—"

"I'm sorry Jack!" the woman cried out. "My family... They threatened my family."

Caine guessed what had happened. But he had no time to react. He heard a loud hiss... a trail of smoke streaked towards them from a nearby hanger.

Rocket-propelled grenade, he thought.

He ducked as the rocket shot over them. A split second later, he realized they were not the projectile's targets.

The Cessna exploded in a fiery inferno. A thousand fragments of burning metal screamed past them through the air. Then the concussion wave hit. The burning hot wind rippled through their clothes and hair, then threw them to the ground.

The tarmac rushed up at Caine.

He hit the ground hard. The fire and heat were replaced by a cold, black darkness.

When he came to he was still lying on the pavement where he had fallen. His ears rang. His head felt like it was clamped in a vice. He tried to move but his body wouldn't respond. A bright light shone in his eyes.

He blinked, then realized the blinding orb was the sun.

A tall, wiry man stared down at him. His features were a blank silhouette... The light fell from behind him, casting a shadow over Caine.

He leaned closer. Caine recognized the man instantly.

The sicario with the face like a grinning skull. The man he had scared off in La Paz.

Whoever he was, the man didn't look scared now. He smiled, then stood up straight. His leg lashed out in a swift kick. The blow struck Caine's head.

For the second time in as many minutes, Caine lost consciousness.

CHAPTER SEVENTEEN

Caine's eyes shot open and he gasped for breath. He was awake again, conscious. This time he was sitting upright, bound to a wooden chair by his wrists and ankles. He was naked, his skin covered in sweat. His own sweat.

He glanced around. The room was dark, but after a few seconds his eyes adjusted to the dim light. The place looked old and industrial, like a warehouse or an abandoned factory. The heat was stifling. The air carried a musty smell... dirt, trash, rotting food. There was an underlying odor of animal feces, and mangy animal fur. He strained against his bindings, but after a few minutes he had to stop struggling. His head throbbed, and his body still ached from the concussion wave of the explosion. His flesh was covered with tiny burns, and bruises where he had bounced on the tarmac.

Could be worse, he thought. *Nothing broken, at least.*

He blinked a couple of times and tried to focus, taking in his surroundings. The empty warehouse was constructed of wooden walls and rafters. He noticed a spattering of brown stains on the floor.

Dried blood, mixed with feces...

Whatever this building was, it didn't take Caine long to figure out its purpose now. This was a slaughterhouse. He knew it wouldn't be long before his own blood joined the old stains on the floor.

He flexed his hands and wrists. They were bound tight behind his back. So were his ankles. The rough cord bit into his flesh.

A man stepped out of the shadows. It was him... the skeleton-faced sicario from La Paz and the airport. He wore dark pants, polished dress shoes and a white business shirt. The clothes fit loosely on his thin frame. But his arms weren't frail or thin. They bulged with lean, taut muscle. As the man moved into the light, Caine saw a cold glimmer in his coal-black eyes. He knew the look well. He had seen it many times, staring back at him in the mirror.

This man was a killer. But unlike Caine, his vicious grin suggested that killing was a pastime he enjoyed.

"Thomas Caine," the man said in a low, rasping voice. *"Bienvenido al infeierno*... welcome to Hell."

Caine glared back at the man. He forced himself not to tremble, not to show fear. He knew few people could hold out for long when faced with torture, and he was no different. It would only be so long before he broke. But until then, he refused to give the man the satisfaction of seeing him cower.

He glanced around the room again. He saw no sign of Jack Tyler. Caine was alone.

The sicario took another step closer, then stopped. Caine grit his teeth. The man was just far enough away that Caine couldn't reach him with a head-butt.

"You and I are both professionals, no?" the man hissed through yellowing teeth.

Caine merely stared at him with his burning green eyes. He did not answer.

"I know you are, Caine. So let us not waste time. If you cooperate, I will make your death painless. On the other hand, if I have to draw the information out of you... Well, then I'm afraid your death will be slow. Slow, and so very painful."

Caine gave his best impression of a confident grin. He knew what was coming. He had been trained for this. But there were some things no training on earth could prepare you for...

"Now that we are clear on the rules, Caine, let me explain what I need—"

"Trust me. I know exactly what you need," Caine snarled through gritted teeth.

The man grinned. His jagged teeth and wide grin made his resemblance to a human skull even more pronounced. "A funny man, no? But believe me, soon it will be I who is laughing."

Caine tugged at his restraints again. They had been expertly knotted. He was only getting free if he could find a means to cut them. He let his head loll forward, his eyes searching the floor for anything sharp.

The man grabbed Caine's chin and jerked his head up. "I only want to know one thing, Caine. Can you guess what that is?"

Caine remained silent. He knew it didn't matter what he said. The sicario would torture him whether he talked or not.

"Tell me where Su Liao is." the man whispered. "That's all I need to know. Nothing more. Nothing complicated."

Caine eyeballed his torturer. He tensed his muscles against his bindings again. His wrists throbbed as the cords bit deeper.

The man stepped back. He paced around Caine, drumming his fingers against his lips. "What to do? Where shall we begin? Electricity? It's simple, leaves no lasting damage... at first." He looked at Caine closely. When he saw no reaction, he shook his head. "No. Not electricity. That doesn't scare you, does it?"

He disappeared into the shadows. The room fell silent, and Caine thought that he was alone again. Then he heard a large object, scraping across the floor. The skeletal man reappeared in the light, dragging a wooden table from some dark corner of the building. The surface of the table was littered with filthy, rusted tools. Hammers, saws, wrenches... common items in any handyman's shed. But here, in this dark, stinking warehouse, Caine knew they had a far more sinister purpose.

The man studied Caine again. "Now, where were we?"

Caine took a deep breath. It was coming. The first pain would be inconsequential, but it would build. If he didn't find a means to escape soon, the tortures would reach a point where his body would be broken, damaged. Then there would be no chance for escape. He had to act now.

The man pointed to a screwdriver, then looked back at Caine. Unsatisfied with Caine's blank stare, he pointed to another tool. A pair of pliers.

"These then? No, perhaps not," he said to himself in a sing song voice.

He pointed to a hammer.

Suddenly his eyes lit up. He had seen something in Caine's expression... Something that had excited him.

"Yes, Caine, a hammer." Spittle flew from his lips as he lifted the tool and weighed it in his hand. "An excellent choice. A hammer can wound you, bruise you. Or it can break every bone in your body. Let us start with the hammer."

Without warning he swung the tool hard, smashing it into Caine's left thigh. The sudden burst of pain felt like the impact of a bullet. Despite his best efforts, Caine cried out as a large purple bruise spread across his flesh. He gritted his teeth, and tried to get his breathing under control. He forced himself to block out the pain. The blow had hurt, but he realized nothing was broken. His torturer was going to take his time. He was going to break Caine apart slowly, piece by piece.

Somewhere in the distance, he heard another man scream.

Caine wasn't certain, but he thought it was Tyler.

The skeletal man smiled again. "You hear that? My men are following my instructions."

Caine glared back at the sadistic killer.

"Let me explain," the man said in his low, rasping whisper. "Each time you scream out, my men will hurt your friend." He flicked the hammer back and forth in his hands. "One of you will surrender to the pain, sooner or later. It is inevitable. One of you will tell me where to find Su Liao. The man who tells me first will have my mercy. I will kill him quickly. But the other will suffer... If it is you, then I will smash every bone in your body to pieces with this hammer. It will take a long time, I think. A long time to die."

He swung the hammer into Caine's left forearm. The knife wound there had not yet healed, and the pain was excruciating. Caine tensed his muscles, breathing deep and fast to control the agony. But once again, he grunted in pain.

Within seconds Tyler screamed again.

The sicario stepped back, taking a break. "Caine," he said through labored breaths, "you and I are alike." He spoke as if they were friends enjoying a pleasant conversation. "You have skills, training. You were special forces, yes?" He watched Caine's expression. "Let me guess? Green Beret?"

Caine looked away. His eyes searched the room again, looking for anything sharp.

"You think someone will come to rescue you?" The man made a clicking noise with his tongue. "You are wrong. No one is coming, Caine."

Caine focused on every corner of the floor not covered in shadow.

Finally, his eyes spotted something... A broken tooth, about five feet away from him.

The man snapped his fingers in Caine's face. "Are you paying attention, gringo? We can keep doing this the hard way, if you like. I don't mind. It's no skin off my back."

Caine tensed up again, but the cords had no give.

The sicario moved around Caine and checked on the bindings. "As I was saying, we are both ex-special forces. I was AFEUR, Colombian Special Forces Group."

The man paced again, walking circles in the dark room. "I know men like you and I are trained to ignore pain, to push through it. That's why, when I torture you today, I will need to inflict far more pain than I would on anyone else. You will suffer more than any man who has been here before you."

Caine watched the man, waiting until he stood in just the right spot. Then he spoke. "You want to find what you have lost?"

The skeletal man stopped. He appeared surprised. "You disappoint me, Mr. Caine. Giving in so soon?"

Caine nodded. "Never liked hammers."

The man grinned. "Go on? Tell me where she is?"

"She? I was talking about your balls, asshole." Caine barked a short, pained laugh. "I saw them at your puta of a mother's house. Right next to the dresser, where I left her some pesos."

Caine was taunting the man now, hoping to force him to lose control. Judging by the fury in the sicario's eyes, it was working.

"Didn't you know? She still keeps them pickled in a jar. Shows them to visitors. She told me she really wanted a girl, not a little *marica* like yourself."

Caine's words had the desired effect. In a fit of rage the man kicked Caine's chair, sending him sprawling onto the muck-stained floor. The impact shocked his aching body, but it was nothing compared to the hammer blows. He groaned, playing up the pain as he writhed on the dirty floor. Behind his back, his fingers grasped at the broken tooth. He slipped it between his thumb and forefinger as the sicario yanked the chair upright.

The skeletal man's face was bright red, and his eyes simmered with rage. He lifted the hammer, aiming the tool at Caine's jaw.

"If you don't want to talk," the man rasped, "then I will make sure you never speak again!"

Caine closed his eyes and prepared for the impact.

When nothing happened, he looked up.

An eerie, serene look filled the man's face. His skin went pale again, as the blood rage drained from his features. He chuckled. "You think you could fool me so easily, eh?"

"If the shoe fits," Caine muttered.

"No. I will not let you end things so quickly. I will enjoy my time with you." He swung the hammer again. The metal head slammed into Caine's right calf.

Caine screamed. Water filled his eyes, and his breath became ragged. And yet, Caine knew this was nothing compared with what was still to come.

Again, Tyler screamed out from a distant room in the same building.

Caine clenched his jaw. He had to control himself if there was any chance of saving his partner.

His only consolation was that now he had the tooth. As he panted for breath, he used his fingers to saw it back and forth behind his back. The jagged edge of the shattered tooth cut at the cord that bound his wrists.

"You can't reach Su Liao," Caine growled through gritted teeth and the sweat pouring off his face. "You'll never find her."

"Don't be so sure about that. We have people everywhere."

"Sure you do."

Suddenly, a door flung open. A beam of light from outside pierced the shadows.

A large man barreled into the room. He was hairy and fat. Caine's eyes opened wide with surprise. Whoever he was, he was dressed like a cowboy. He wore a gold-plated .357 Magnum revolver at his waist. The gun's holster was decorated with gleaming metal wolves. It matched a wolf's head belt buckle, also forged in gold. His sweating face was covered by a scraggly beard. His clothes looked expensive and freshly ironed.

"Supay," the fat man said in a calm but commanding voice.

Supay lowered his hammer and stood up. "Yes Jefe?" he answered in respect of his boss. Caine sensed an edge of contempt in his voice.

"Forget this gringo, Supay. He is of no use."

Supay shook his head. "I disagree Jefe. Caine, or his friend in the next room, can lead us to Su Liao. Unless she is eliminated, she could compromise our operation."

The other man patted Supay on the back. "No. Supay. I just got word Su Liao was seen at Miami airport, two days ago. She was whisked away in a government convoy. She is beyond our reach now."

"But the rendezvous, in Los Angeles. They will know about that—"

"That can all be changed. We will arrange a new drop off point when you meet with Zhao."

Caine listened as he sawed at his bindings. He suspected that when this conversation ended, they would waste no more time. They'd execute him quickly. He had to be ready to act.

Supay's black eyes narrowed. "I should have killed the whore in La Paz when I had the chance."

"Yes, you should have. But it matters little now."

"So we just kill this gringo and his friend? Be done with them?"

The fat man nodded. "Yes, but leave them to me. You need to meet with Zhao and the submarine. Time is running out. I will deal with Caine in my... usual way."

Caine frantically rubbed the jagged edge of the tooth across his bindings. As he worked, he kept his eyes on the two men.

"And the bitch?" Supay asked. "Kill her too?"

The Jefe shrugged. "She's going to bleed out soon. Until then, I might as well have some fun with her. Then I'll hand her over to my men to finish her." He patted Supay on the back again. "Smile, my friend. Everything we have planned will soon come to pass. You and I will be rich."

The fat man glanced over Supay's shoulder and stared at Caine. "And these fools will soon learn of the legend... They will die begging for mercy, as El Lobizon feasts on their blood."

CHAPTER EIGHTEEN

Caine's eyes followed Supay as he left the torture chamber. As the skeletal man's footsteps echoed in the distance, Caine sawed at his bonds with the shattered tooth. He had to work fast, not just to save himself, but Valencia and Tyler too. The woman had betrayed them, but he knew she was not his enemy. The cartel had forced her hand by threatening her family. If he could somehow get them all out of this mess, she could still be a valuable ally.

With Supay gone, the fat cartel boss turned to Caine and grinned. "Time to finish you." Spit gathered on the edge of his bulbous lips.

Caine was nowhere near close to cutting his bonds. He had to keep the fat man talking. "I thought he was the boss?" Caine taunted.

The man's eyes grew dark and narrow. "Do you know who I am?"

"Actually, I do."

"Then say my name."

Caine chuckled. "You're Enrique Rojas."

The words caused the fat man to tense. His brows bunched, revealing his annoyance. "That is not my name."

"Sure it is," Caine replied with a smile.

During his down time at Langley, Caine read every situation report that passed through his inbox. The heads of various Latin American drug cartels were a common subject. He had memorized most of their names. He knew Rojas was a mid-level player in the Colombian underworld. The drug lord controlled cocaine manufacturing and distribution around Tumaco. He paid a share of his profits as protection money to the larger cartels in Bogota, Cali and Medellin.

The fat man glared at him, then spat on the floor. "Stupid *gringo*. Have you not heard the legend? My name is—"

"Yeah, Yeah, I know. El Lobizon. Enough with the ghost stories. We both know your real name is Enrique Rojas."

According to the files Rebecca had provided him in Peru, everyone operating in the intelligence or judicial system with an interest in Tumaco knew of Rojas' obsession... The myth of El Lobizon. The Latin American fairytale was similar to European werewolf myths. Besides, it was not like the man kept his alter-ego identity secret. Quite the opposite, in fact.

Rojas' face twisted into a mask of fury. He gnashed his teeth, and a vein popped out on his forehead. "It doesn't matter, Caine. You'll be dead in minutes."

Caine forced himself to laugh. "What are you going to do? Transform into a wolf, and eat me?"

The hulking man's lip quivered. He clenched his fists, barely able to contain his rage.

Meanwhile, Caine continued cutting his bindings.

"This is South America," Rojas growled. "We may have adopted Catholicism, but that doesn't mean we gave up the old ways of the Incans, the Moche or the Tiwanaku. The tribes of the Amazon share blood with us here. Their medicine men brew potions that alter the mind, Caine. The people believe in witches and demons, monsters and spirits—"

"Go on then," Caine taunted. "Might as well see the show before I die. Show me the legend. Show me El Lobizon."

"You will see soon enough."

Caine snorted. "You're pathetic, Rojas. Not to mention a fake."

Rojas punched Caine hard in the gut.

Caine was ready for it. He tightened his abdominal muscles as the blow struck. He held the tooth safely behind his back until the pain faded, then he resumed sawing at the ropes.

"It doesn't matter what I believe," said the flabby cartel leader. "Or what Gringos like you believe. It only matters that my enemies and the scared sheep in this town believe. If they fear I am a wolf, then I become a wolf in their minds. If they fear I am El Lobizon, then I am El Lobizon. Fear gives men like me power."

"You got that last bit right. Without fear, you're nothing, Rojas. Just another two-bit drug dealer south of the border. In a year or two, someone else will come along. Someone younger, hungrier. The people will have a new monster to worry about. They'll forget your little legend soon enough."

Rojas punched Caine in the mouth. The blow rattled Caine's jaw. He tasted blood, but his teeth remained intact.

When Caine recovered, he tested his bindings again. They had a little give now. He was almost through.

"I will set my dogs on you," Rojas panted. His breath was heavy with anger and rage. "Everyone will hear them rip you and your friend to pieces. Then they will feed on your meat and lick up every last drop of your blood. And everyone will know who butchered you. El Lobizon. The monster that haunts the nightmares of children. They will know, and they will believe. Just as you will soon believe."

Caine kept cutting. He was almost there. "Sorry Rojas. I don't believe in fairytales."

"We will see, Caine. We will see."

Rojas exited the room. Caine heard him with his dogs. They howled and snarled in the dark recesses of the warehouse. He assumed Rojas was beating them with a stick, enraging the poor beasts. The drug lord had likely starved them as well, so they would make quick work of their victims.

Caine worked faster. He felt the bindings around his wrists go loose. He flexed his arms, and the thin, frayed cord snapped. His hands were free.

The sore muscles in his legs burned in agony as he shot to his feet. He ignored the pain, slipping the cords that bound his ankles off the chair legs. A door in the shadows creaked opened.

A large Doberman pinscher paced into the room. It stood growling in the dim light. It advanced cautiously, one heavy paw after the other. It was stalking Caine, closing in for the kill.

Naked and vulnerable, Caine crouched and stepped backwards.

The animal sensed his fear. It bared its fangs and uttered a vicious snarl. Then it charged.

The savage dog was upon him in seconds, its jaws snapping and biting at his naked flesh. Caine's leg swung out. He heard the dog yelp as he kicked it hard in the ribs. The animal fell to the floor. Caine kicked it again, and heard the crack of breaking bones.

The dog picked itself up off the ground. It whimpered, and limped forward a few steps. Then it snarled, and leapt at Caine once more.

As much as Caine hated hurting animals, he had no choice. It was him or the beast. He locked his fingers together and pummeled the savage animal with a double fisted blow. He heard more ribs break as his fists thudded into the beast's flesh.

He swung an arm around the animal's neck, pinning it in a lock.

The dog struggled. Its paws clawed at the floor. It fought to live, as all animals did.

But Caine was stronger. His grip around the dog was crushing its windpipe. It took a while to die. Thirty seconds. Maybe a minute. Eventually the poor animal's brain was exhausted of oxygen. Its paws slowed their frantic scratching. Its body hung limp in Caine's arms.

He dropped the canine to the floor. Then he marched out of the room and into the darkness beyond.

In the shadows, he saw a terrified Enrique Rojas backing away from him. He had just watched Caine butcher his alter-ego. He was desperately trying to load bullets from his belt into the gold-plated Magnum revolver. The gun shook in his hands. He dropped a few bullets, and they rolled across the floor.

As Caine moved closer, Rojas managed to load the gun. He snapped the cylinder closed, and raised the revolver in a one handed grip. He was too late.

Caine snatched the weapon from his hand. He flipped open the cylinder, and checked to be sure it was loaded. Then spun the chamber closed, and placed the weapon on the so-called werewolf's head.

"Please, wait," the fat man gasped. "I can pay you, I can—"

"Let's find out if the legends are true," Caine snarled.

He inhaled, and held his breath. Then he squeezed the trigger.

Rojas' head exploded in a shower of bone and brain matter. Half his face disintegrated into a pink cloud, as the fat corpse fell onto the filthy floor.

There were two more dogs in the cages. Both leapt at the bars, growling and snapping at Caine. He knew Rojas had trained them to be vicious. Tortured them, beat them…

Caine hated himself for what he was about to do, but he had no choice. He fired a bullet into the skull of each animal, putting them out of their misery.

As the second shot echoed through the room, another door burst open. A naked, muscular man rushed in, bellowing an unintelligible war cry. He pointed a glimmering knife at Caine as he charged across the floor.

Caine spun around, aiming the Magnum revolver at the new intruder.

It was Tyler! Jack's body was bloody and beaten, and several burns marked his skin. But he was alive.

Tyler's eyes opened wide with surprise. He lowered the knife, and glanced at the corpse on the ground.

"Damn Caine! I thought I was about to save your ass," Tyler said through a grin.

"I was about to do the same for you."

Tyler nodded. "Right, well let's save the high fives for later. We need to clear the building. And find some fucking clothes, before any more of these jokers show up."

"That's not all," Caine said, taking a second to catch his breath. "Your friend Valencia is still alive. We need to find her too."

CHAPTER NINETEEN

The two operatives covered each other as they swept through the rest of the dark warehouse. As they stalked past another room, Caine noticed three male corpses sprawled across the floor inside. Their throats were slit, and dark liquid pooled around their bodies. Tyler's handiwork, no doubt. He knew the former Delta Force operator was skilled with a knife.

When they were satisfied no one else was in the building, Caine and Tyler searched for their missing clothes. They finally found their torn, stained garments stuffed in a trash bag in a dingy corridor. Caine dressed first while Tyler kept an eye out for attackers. Then Tyler did the same while Caine provided cover.

They found Valencia in a cell. She too had been stripped naked except for a dirty bandage around her thigh. She was tied to a metal frame bed on a moldy mattress stained with old blood, and flinched when the door burst open. Her fear was quickly replaced with relief when she saw Tyler.

"Valencia, you okay?" Tyler asked as he cut her bindings.

She sat up and rubbed her wrists. "I'll live," she muttered. As she shifted her legs, a hiss of pain escaped her lips. She pulled down the bandage and checked her wound. The bullet seemed to have gone right through the muscle. It wasn't bleeding much, but the wound was red with infection. "You're a good shot," she said to Caine through gritted teeth. She looked up at him. "I assume you weren't trying to kill me. The wound is through and through."

"I made a split second decision," Caine muttered. "Glad it was the right one.

"I think it's infected though," she said, her face a grimace of pain. "This shithole isn't exactly sterile. Gonna need some antibiotics." When neither man said a word, she glanced down at her sweating, naked body. "Some clothes would be nice too."

"Right," Caine said, averting his eyes. "I'm on it." He felt like he was moving in slow motion. A thick haze clouded his thoughts. The adrenaline rush of the last hour was wearing off... He had been acting on instinct and muscle memory until now. The sharp, stinging agony of the hammer blows had shifted to a dull, throbbing ache. He knew the pain would not go away anytime soon. But he had to push through.

They were not yet safe.

"Caine," Tyler added before he left. "I'll stay here with Valencia and check this wound."

Caine nodded, then left the room and searched the warehouse. Eventually he found their wallets and passports, along with Valencia's police badge and car keys. He finally found her clothes as well, piled on a battered wooden table. Unfortunately, their weapons were nowhere to be seen. After scouring the entire building, the closest thing to medicine he could fine was a half-empty bottle of tequila.

He returned to find Tyler examining Valencia's wound. "Well, she's right. The bullet went straight through, missed the bone and major arteries."

"It still hurts like hell," Valencia gasped.

Caine handed over the tequila. "This is the best I can do for now. Pour it over the wound. It should clean it out."

Tyler took the bottle and splashed the alcohol on both the entry and exit holes. Valencia cried out as he worked on her. Tyler tore the sleeves off his shirt and wrapped them around the wound as a makeshift bandage. Then he helped her dress.

"Time to move," Tyler commanded.

Valencia leaned on Tyler as Caine led them out of the building. Outside the blazing sun overhead was harsh and bright. After being locked in the dark for so long, the light was blinding. When their eyes adjusted to the glare, they found themselves on the streets of Tumaco. The pavement was cracked and broken. The neighboring buildings were colorful but decrepit. Their rusted, corrugated iron roofs sloped inward, collapsing under their own weight. Piles of rubble blocked the sidewalks, and a tangle of humming wires criss-crossed over their heads.

"I know where we are," Valencia said. "My car is not far from here."

They hobbled down a few streets until they reached Valencia's battered Toyota Landcruiser. The keys Caine had grabbed in the warehouse opened the door. He drove while Tyler used the vehicle's first aid kit to do a better job at treating Valencia's wound.

"What now?" she asked.

"Now we do what we came for," Caine said, keeping an eye on the dusty streets outside. "I have the coordinates where the Chinese sub is supposed to collect the cocaine shipment."

"Chinese submarine? What are you talking about?" Valencia asked.

"China's working with the Columbian drug cartels. Or at least a rogue sub commander is," Caine said as they spun around a corner. "I need weapons and a speedboat if I'm going to stop them."

"Can you give me the coordinates?" she asked.

Caine paused. He knew the woman had no choice; her family had been threatened. But still...

She betrayed you, whispered a voice in the back of his head. *You should cut her loose, now. She can't be trusted...*

Tyler glanced up at him. His piercing blue eyes met Caine's

emerald stare in the rearview mirror. He seemed to know what Caine was thinking.

"She can help, Caine."

He spun the wheel, turning the car down another narrow, crumbling street. He glanced at the woman in the backseat, then repeated the coordinates from memory.

"That's about fifteen kilometers northwest of here," she replied. "Out in the Pacific Ocean."

Caine glanced at the clock on the car. According to Su Liao's information, he had about an hour before the transaction took place. "Doesn't give me a lot of time."

"Doesn't give us a lot of time, you mean" Tyler said with mock indignation.

"Jack, you have to get Valencia to a hospital. She needs proper medical treatment, and you need to check on her family. After that, I need you to get back to the airport."

Tyler frowned. "Why the airport?"

"That submarine carries six torpedoes. Until they load the cocaine, each one of those tubes is capable of firing. I need an exfil plan that doesn't involve water. Otherwise I'm a sitting duck."

"Got it. Roger that."

Valencia shifted in her seat. She lifted a tarp in the back of the Landcruiser revealing Glock 19 pistols and M16A2 assault rifles. "You'll need these," she said calmly.

"That's my girl!" Tyler said. He grabbed one of the assault rifles, slotted in a magazine, then chambered a round. He passed a pistol and assault rifle up to Caine, along with several spare magazines. "It's like Christmas morning!"

"I'll need transportation. A speedboat, something fast," Caine said.

The woman smiled. "I can help with that too. Turn right at the next intersection."

Valencia directed him to a jetty at the edge of town. Several brightly colored speedboats bobbed in the green water, moored to a rickety wooden dock.

Caine parked the vehicle, and leapt out the driver's side door. Tyler scrambled into the front seat, and grabbed the wheel. "Good luck Caine," he said through the open window. "See you in a few!"

He gunned the engine and tore off. Caine watched as the Landcruiser vanished in a cloud of dust, heading back towards the heart of Tumaco.

Then he turned and raced down the jetty, assault rifle at the ready. He spotted a luxury speedboat tied off near the end of the dock. The sleek vessel was thirty-six feet in length, and sported dual 250 horsepower engines.

Exactly what he needed.

A pair of men wearing open Hawaiian shirts and tight speedo bathing suits sat in the back of the boat. They were pulling frosted cans of beer from a crumpled box, and looked up in surprise as Caine charged up to the boat.

Caine pointed his assault rifle at the presumed owners. They dropped their beers and raised their hands. The cans bounced across the deck, shooting jets of pressurized alcohol into the air.

Caine sized the pair up as he peered down the rifle's barrel. A chunky, gold watch sparkled on one of the men's wrists. Expensive watch, speed boat... *Drug dealers*, he thought. *Maybe smugglers*. No one else could afford this stuff.

"Sorry, amigos," Caine growled, "I need to borrow your boat."

The men crawled up onto the jetty, keeping their hands raised in the air. Caine turned the starter, and the engines growled to life. He cast off the mooring ropes, keeping the rifle trained on the two men. Then he got behind the wheel, pushed the throttle forward, and sped out into the open water. As the boat angled towards the ocean, it drenched the dock in a spray of water.

He quickly left the jetty in his wake. Once he was beyond the sand bars and river mouth, the water grew dark and choppy. Caine checked the GPS coordinates on the boat's navigation system. He turned northwest, following the course Su Liao had given him.

He hoped her intel would prove reliable.

Caine squinted as the sun's golden kiss reflected off the rippling water. The salt spray stung his skin as the bow bounced across the water. Behind him, the twin motors roared like angry beasts.

The noise didn't bother him. At this point, stealth was not a part of his plans.

Besides, he thought, *if Su Liao's coordinates are right, things are about to get even louder...*

CHAPTER TWENTY

COLOMBIAN TERRITORIAL WATERS, PACIFIC OCEAN

Captain Zhao Jianyu stood on the deck of the *Hai Long*, watching three 'go-fast' speedboats approach from the southeast. He knew each cartel vessel was loaded with bags of pure cocaine. They also carried a crew of Colombian thugs, armed with outdated knock-off U.S. weaponry. The men were there to oversee the transfer of drugs to his submarine.

Zhao stood ramrod straight, and held his hands clasped behind his back. The faintest hint of a smile curled across his lips.

Soon, he thought... *Soon all my planning and sacrifice will bear fruit. My mission, my true mission, will be a success.*

His only regret was that no one would ever know... When he pulled this off, it would be the largest single shipment of pure cocaine ever to enter the United States of America. He would flood the market. Street prices would drop. More Americans than ever would turn to the illicit drug, saddling more of the population with a crippling addiction. In his own way, he was striking a blow against the country, making it just that little bit more ineffective.

But more importantly, he would become rich. Wealthier than he had ever dreamed possible.

The shimmering boats streaked closer, leaving white trails across the water. Zhao glanced back at his men. For his own protection, several sailors were stationed on deck, carrying QBZ-95 Assault Rifles and QCW-05 Assault Guns. He had illegally stowed the weapons onboard for this mission.

His men had even mounted a QW-1 Vanguard man-portable air-defense system to a bracket on the conning tower. The weapon had required several exorbitant bribes to secure, but the extra firepower was worth it. Zhao had little reason to trust El Lobizon's men. And even if the Cartel didn't prove to be a problem, the *Hai Long* was vulnerable when surfaced. Colombian or United States' naval or air forces could appear at any moment.

To mitigate the risk, he didn't intend to stay surfaced for long. The plan was simple... load the almost ten tons of pure cocaine into the torpedo tubes as quickly as possible, then dive and head for California. Every second counted, and he had drilled his men relentlessly on the journey to this point.

Like silver bullets, the go-fast boats screamed across the water. They moved faster than any vessel Zhao had ever seen. As they neared the floating submarine, their motors finally died down, and they slowed to a halt. One of the chugging boats drifted close enough to pull alongside the *Hai Long*. Zhao knew the other two vessels would hang back until they knew everything was proceeding as planned. Both sides were cautious.

One of the thugs on the boat threw a rope to Zhao's men. They expertly tied it off, allowing the vessel to berth alongside the larger submarine. A gaunt, pale-faced man climbed onto the deck of the Type 093 prototype submarine. He wore a white long sleeve shirt, matching pants, and polished boots. Zhao spotted the butt of a pistol tucked into the back of his pants, the only visible weapon he carried.

The man turned to face Zhao. Up close, he looked even paler. His face was as white as a corpse and his eyes were two dark pools of ink. There was something about the way he moved, and his eyes darted over Zhao's men, observing everything around him. Zhao gritted his teeth. This man was not like the others. He was military trained... He was dangerous.

"I'm Supay," he said, introducing himself in English in a harsh, almost whispery growl. English was the only language they both understood, which was fine with Zhao. The last thing he wanted to hear was this hired gun's mangled attempts at speaking Chinese.

"I know who you are," Zhao snapped. "Carlos Supay. I was expecting your superior."

"He trusts me with the details of the mission," Supay answered, his voice calm and smug. "He could not be with us today, as he's busy fixing a problem you should have dealt with yourself."

Zhao paused, aware his men were watching him for any pre-arranged signals. If Zhao's hands touched his face, that meant he didn't trust the Colombians. In which case, his men had orders to shoot every last one of them dead. He almost touched his face in that moment. Instead, he asked, "And what problem is that?"

"The girl. Su Liao. You said she was not a threat."

"She isn't," Zhao responded calmly. "She provided the fake path across the Pacific which we are transmitting back to Beijing even now. Holding her parents in one of our reeducation camps was exactly the persuasion she required to do her job. She'll keep her mouth shut."

Supay's eyes grew even darker. "But she didn't, Zhao," he hissed through gritted teeth. "She was in Bolivia two days ago, finalizing her defection to America."

Zhao struggled to hide his surprise. A tremor ran across his lips, and his eyes narrowed. He was stunned by this revelation. He had made it clear to Su Liao that if she did not do exactly as instructed, her parents would be tortured in the most horrific means possible. Then they would be executed.

His face flushed red. He clenched his fists behind his back. He was enraged by her audacity, by her will to defy him. "I do hope for your sake, Supay, that you have her in your custody."

Supay shook his head. "No. Three CIA agents snatched Liao right from under our noses. Luckily we captured two of the Americans. They are both dead now. But they revealed Su Liao was already in America. She is under U.S. Government protection."

"Then you should have killed her when you had the chance," Zhou shouted.

"If you had taken care of her in the first place, we wouldn't have this problem," Supay hissed back.

The two furious men stared at each other in silence. Finally, Supay licked his lips, and spoke. "To ensure there are no further fuck ups, I'm coming with you."

Every muscle in Zhao's body tensed involuntarily. "What?"

The skeletal-faced man nodded. "You've let us down. Me, and one man of my choosing, will board your submarine. We will ensure the merchandise makes it to California as agreed."

Zhao's fists clenched in anger, cracking his knuckles. "If you let Liao escape, she will know where the shipment rendezvous will be, and tell the Americans—"

"We've already changed the pick-up location and the time," Supay interrupted. "To ensure there are no more difficulties, you will only be told the precise coordinates once we are on our way."

Zhao considered these new demands. Despite his anger, they seemed reasonable enough. If Supay and his man proved problematic, it would not be difficult for his sailors to murder them and toss their bodies into the sea. But he doubted it would come to that. Seeing this mission through to its profitable conclusion was in both their best interests.

But there was still one thing Zhao couldn't understand. Why had Su Liao defied him? She was weak... she was nothing. It infuriated him that a mere woman was complicating his plans.

"We load the cocaine now," Supay insisted. "The time for talk is over."

Zhao once again considered touching his face, giving the order to have the Colombians murdered here and now. His men could still load the cocaine onboard, still take it to America. The only problem was, Zhao had no idea who to sell it too. He needed a buyer.

No. Zhao decided he had to continue with this relationship for now. The wealth and the power it would bring him was more important than losing a little pride over this momentary annoyance.

"Zhao?" Supay asked again. "I said we—"

"Fine. I accept your conditions—"

A sailor interrupted them. "Captain, there's another vessel heading this way. It's coming in fast!"

"Is that one of yours?" Zhao asked.

Supay turned. He squinted, trying to identify who piloted the boat roaring across the water. He seemed to recognize the man in the speedboat tearing at breakneck speed towards them.

"No," Supay said, his voice cold as ice. "That's one of the American spies."

"I thought they were dead?"

"I made a mistake." Supay pulled his pistol from his belt and racked the slide, chambering the first round. "I won't make the same mistake twice."

CHAPTER TWENTY-ONE

Caine powered the speedboat through the choppy waters, pushing the odometer to sixty miles per hour. He could see the submarine now, and three custom-made go-fast boats moored nearby. The long, narrow go-fasts were the latest tool in the drug cartels' arsenal. Each boat was custom-built for speed, designed to outrun Coast Guard and Naval vessels as they smuggled cocaine into the United States. If it came to a chase, Caine knew his boat would be no match against them in speed or maneuverability.

As he sped closer, he spotted frantic activity on the deck of the submarine. The criminals must have seen him by now. Caine ducked low behind the dashboard. He knew what was coming.

A split-second later, bullets ricocheted off the bow. The sloped windshield exploded above him, raining glass shards over his body. There was a brief pause, then a second hail of gunfire struck the boat. Caine pushed on, piloting the boat towards a gap between two of the go-fasts anchored nearby. The engines roared even louder as he increased his speed. His free hand gripped a five-gallon drum of fuel, one of four he had readied earlier.

The bursts of enemy gunfire fire continued. Wood splinters

exploded from the bow, as the bullets perforated his vessel's hull. Caine pushed the throttle hard. The boat leapt forward, charging directly towards the closest enemy vessel. The men on board sent one last hail of bullet's exploding towards Caine, but they were too late. They screamed and threw themselves to the deck, as Caine's boat roared closer.

CRASH!

For a moment, the shriek of torn wood and metal drowned out the sound of the engines. The impact reverberated through the hull, sending a shockwave of pain through his bones. As his speedboat exploded over the top of the savaged go-fast, Caine hurled the first fuel drum onto their deck. Then he grabbed the side of his boat, as he slammed back into the water with a mighty splash.

The criminals in the crippled boat staggered to their feet. As they spun around and took aim at the fleeing boat, a haze of diesel fumes filled the air around them.

Before they could counter-attack, Caine spun around and opened fire. His rifle sent a barrage of bullets into the slick of fuel spreading across the deck. Sparks flew as the gunfire struck the boat's hull. The fuel vapors mixed with the surrounding oxygen and ignited, erupting into a glowing fireball. The exploding fuel canister flew through the air like a rocket, burying itself in the cabin of the go-fast. Dancing tongues of orange flame engulfed the charred remains of the boat. Caine heard the men onboard screaming as the fire burned them alive. Their cries faded as he sped further away from the burning wreckage.

Caine pushed the throttle forward. He raised his head, glancing over the splintered bow. The go-fast on his starboard side rocked up and down in the water. The explosion he had triggered had sent massive vibrations through the water. The men on the other boat were struggling to maintain their balance as the sea churned around them. Caine ignored them and plowed towards the third go-fast. The boat was moored to the submarine, and its crew were frantically unloading bundles of cocaine.

Caine ducked down again. The Chinese sailors opened fire with their assault rifles. They attacked with military discipline, taking turns peppering his boat with fresh volleys of bullets. With each ping of metal on metal, Caine knew his speedboat was taking more damage. It wouldn't last much longer.

Without warning, a blast of white smoke erupted from the deck of the submarine. A bright streak flew through the air, heading towards Caine's boat.

Caine spotted it just in time. He yanked hard on the wheel. Water sloshed over the deck as he spun the boat into a tight turn. As he sped out of the projectile's path, he felt a wave of heat rush over him.

A second later the missile struck the water.

The explosion was loud and bright. A plume of water erupted into the air. The shockwaves pushed Caine's boat forward. He rammed into the submarine, splintering more of the wood on his bow. The impact threw Caine forward, and his head struck the console. He tasted blood, but ignored the pain. His vision faded. The sound of bullets and the sloshing of the water sounded muted, distant. As if they were far away, echoing through a long, dark tunnel.

Caine wiped the blood and sweat from his eyes. He staggered back onto his feet, remembering his insane plan.

Got to keep moving, he thought. *Keep them reacting.*

He drew his pistol and fired several rounds towards the sailors up on deck. As they scrambled for cover, he opened the next fuel drum and hurled it onto the deck of the Chinese vessel. Then he aimed his pistol at the fuel spilling out of the ruptured drum.

Before he could fire, a dark shape leapt from the deck of the submarine. The figure slammed into him, knocking the gun from his hands. Caine stumbled backwards as his pistol slid across the deck. His back hit into the throttle lever, and the boat roared away from the submarine.

His attacker rose to his feet. Anger flared in his dark, sunken eyes.

Caine recognized him immediately.

Supay!

The former Colombian special forces soldier didn't speak. He lunged forward, slashing at Caine with a knife.

He knocked Supay's knife aside each time the man thrust forward.

The sicario was agile and well trained. While he failed to wound Caine with his lightning-fast strikes, he continued to press his attack, keeping Caine on the defensive. He slashed again and again, his onslaught relentless. Each man struggled to keep his balance as the speed boat skipped over the waves. The first man to fall would be the first man to die.

Supay thrust again. This time the blade found a gap in Caine's defenses. A crimson gash opened up on Caine's right forearm.

Caine winced, but he kept moving. Stepping backwards, he kicked over another fuel drum. The bouncing motion of the boat sent it rolling towards Supay's legs.

His attacker twisted sideways, but he was too late. The heavy barrel slammed into his knees. Supay stumbled and fell to the ground, smacking his head against the deck. His pupils dilated, and he groaned as he slipped into unconsciousness.

Caine dove for the deck and grabbed his pistol. He steadied himself and aimed the weapon at Supay, ready to send a pair of 9mm rounds into the man's head.

Before he could fire, another impact shook the boat. Caine was knocked off his feet. He grunted as his tailbone slammed into the deck.

Looking up, he saw the hull of another go-fast drifting next to him. The boat had plowed into his port side. The men on board fired their submachine guns as they motored past. Bullets tore across the deck, sweeping towards Caine. He rolled sideways, taking cover behind the pilot's chair.

Caine stayed low, watching the other boat shoot past him in the water. Its speed was incredible. He guessed it was going at least eighty miles per hour or more. It spun around in the distance, turning in a wide circle and angling back towards him.

The hairs on the back of Caine's neck tingled. Blood thundered in his temples. He sensed something had changed on the field of battle.

He spun his gaze back towards the submarine. It was gone.

Must have submerged during the fighting, he thought.

In the bubbling sea where it had previously surfaced, Caine now saw a series of long wave troughs. They lined up one after the other, like arrows, streaking though the water. Something was speeding just under the surface, heading straight towards his boat.

He knew of only one thing that could cause a wave trail like that.

Torpedo...

Caine grabbed the wheel and pushed the throttle to the max. The engines screamed, and smoke began to billow from the stern.

The attacking go-fast raced closer. It had completed its turn, and was coming around for another strafing run.

Caine pointed his bow directly towards it. They were rushing at each other head on. His foes refused to break off. The two boats were on a collision course.

Okay, assholes, he thought. *Let's play chicken...*

He glanced back. The tiny waves were rushing closer to his stern. The torpedo was closing in... he couldn't outrun it.

The go-fast loomed closer through the shattered windshield. Gunfire erupted from the men onboard, peppering Caine's bow. He ducked down below the console, but held his course.

Not yet. Closer... Closer ...

At the last second, Caine threw the wheel to the left. His boat sloshed to the side, narrowly avoiding a collision with the go-fast.

The criminals onboard spun around on the deck, aiming their machine pistols at Caine's side as he sped past. They didn't see the torpedo racing towards them.

Not until it was too late.

KABOOM!

The explosion tossed the go-fast out of the water. The boat flipped three times before it crashed back into the waves, and broke up into fragments. The ocean turned frothing white, then pink. A mixture of cocaine and blood stained the churning waters.

Caine's ears rang from the explosion. He couldn't hear a thing, and his brain felt like it was vibrating inside his skull. The pressure built up behind his temples, until he felt like his eyes were ready to pop. He pushed on, ignoring the pain. The submarine was beneath him somewhere. He knew it would have plenty of torpedoes left in its arsenal.

He heard the scream of another high-speed motor, rushing across the water behind him. The last go-fast was bearing down on him, stalking him across the sea like a hungry cheetah, running down a gazelle.

Caine readied another drum of fuel. He glanced over his shoulders to determine his foes' location. The go-fast was darting and weaving across the water behind him. With a terrifying burst of speed, it accelerated and rammed Caine. The sharp, wedge-shaped prow smashed into one of his motors. Then the sleek boat fell back, as one of his two-fifty horsepower engines disintegrated and tore away.

He glanced down at the controls. The odometer needle dropped. He was losing speed.

He spun around and fired, emptying the magazine in his pistol. Caine hit the hull, but the bullets had little effect. The enemy accelerated again, ready to ram his last engine.

As Caine reloaded his weapon, he saw a fist-sized object fall from the sky and bounce across the go-fast's deck. A second later another explosion tore through the deck of the enemy boat. A fireball devoured the remains of the craft, engulfing the men and the last of the cocaine.

A Cessna plane swooped through the air, banking low over the ocean. As it turned it dropped a rope ladder.

Tyler, Caine thought. He'd managed to secure another plane.

There was only one problem. The Cessna's speed couldn't drop below seventy miles per hour without stalling and crashing into the ocean. And with only one engine remaining, Caine's speedboat would barely get up to fifty miles per hour.

Caine turned to the controls. The loss of the engine had thrown the boat off balance, sending the vessel careening across the water at an angle if he didn't correct with the wheel.

Caine grabbed a boat hook that lay in a trough next to the console. He thrust it into the air, preparing to snag the ladder as Tyler flew by. As the Cessna approached for its first extraction attempt, Caine heard a snarl of anger from the rear of the boat. He spun around.

Supay staggered to his feet. An angry purple bruise marked the side of his forehead, but he was otherwise unharmed.

He bared his teeth, and pointed his knife at Caine. "We have unfinished business, amigo."

He exploded forward, swinging his blade in a wide, deadly arc.

CHAPTER TWENTY-TWO

Supay sliced through the air with the razor-sharp blade. The knife narrowly missed Caine's face. The gaunt man growled, and swung again. Caine parried with the boat hook, barely avoiding another deep cut across his arm.

He swung the hook up, knocking Supay's knife arm aside. Then he thrust forward, slamming the wood shaft of the hook into the skeletal man's face. He heard a sharp crack. Supay stumbled backwards, blood streaming from his broken nose.

As Caine regained his balance, he looked over the shoulder of his attacker. He saw another trough of waves, rushing closer.

A second torpedo was powering through the water towards them.

"You can't win," Caine yelled over the noise of the faltering engine, hoping to distract his foe. The Cessna sped back towards him, following the wake of the torpedo, and racing to reach Caine first. Caine squinted at the plane, estimating its speed and altitude. He only had one chance to survive this, and success depended on too many factors he couldn't control.

"The cocaine is gone," he yelled at Supay. "Zhao left you dead in the water!"

Supay's lips twisted into a maniacal grin. With his crushed nose and sunken eyes, his face looked more skeletal than ever. Caine could barely hear the man's words through the ringing in his ears, and the noise of the boat and the plane.

Supay pointed at him with his knife. "It's not over, Caine. Not until you die!"

The Cessna swooped low overhead, and the dangling ladder flew towards them. Caine held up the hook. He felt it catch, yanking him up off the deck. His shoulder screamed as he whipped through the air. He felt like his arm was tearing from its socket. He reached up with his free hand. His fingers wrapped around the bottom rung of the ladder. He grabbed hold, just as the boat hook lost its grip and fell away into the churning seas.

Caine looked down. The speedboat grew smaller, as the plane carried him higher into the air. He could just make out a shocked and surprised Supay glaring up at him. The white trail of the torpedo cut through the water, arching closer to the boat.

It hit, and the speedboat disintegrated. The water around the vessel seemed to implode for a second, then it blew apart in a mighty wave of churning foam, tossing pieces of wood and metal across the sea. One second the boat was there. The next it was gone, replaced with specks of burning debris.

Caine commenced his slow climb up into the Cessna. The task was difficult, partially from the beating Caine had taken, but more so because of the battering winds. Rung by rung, Caine pulled himself up. As he got higher the climb became easier, for there was less swing in the ladder. After what seemed like an eternity, he pulled himself inside the tiny cabin.

A wide-eyed Julia Valencia helped him in. "Wow!" she shouted over the noise of the engine. The ringing in his ears had lessened. She closed the door, reducing the rattle inside the small six-seater. "I can't believe you pulled that off!"

Caine rolled onto his back wincing in pain. "That makes two of us," he grunted. "Is your family okay?"

She smiled. "Yes. No one was hurt. And now, thanks to you and Jack, El Lobizon will never be able to threaten me again." She kissed him gently on the forehead. "It's almost enough to make me forget you shot me."

Caine laughed, then winced as a jolt of pain shot through his battered body. "Yeah, well you drew first."

She mussed his hair. "Let's try not to make a habit of it."

Caine forced himself to sit up. The bruises and cuts across his body throbbed in agony. He knew it would take some time to physically recover from his ordeal. He looked at Tyler in the cockpit. His partner gave Caine a thumbs up.

"Good job bud!" Tyler shouted over the engine's roar. "Couldn't have done it better myself."

"Thanks." Caine grinned. "Thought I was a dead man there for a second."

"Yeah, so did I."

Caine looked out across the ocean. They flew towards the land, and the vast plain of blue water soon transformed into a haze of green mangroves and rainforests. As the scenery streaked by, Caine closed his eyes.

Within seconds he fell into a deep, dreamless sleep.

CHAPTER TWENTY-THREE

WEST VIRGINIA, UNITED STATES

From the outside, Su Liao's new home seemed like a paradise. The grounds surrounding her safehouse were stunning. The buildings where she worked lay deep within a red pine and spruce forest. Rugged hills rose up in the distance. A creek meandered through the woods, ending at a cascading waterfall.

Su was grateful she could explore the natural beauty when she took breaks from her computer. She could jog, practice her tai chi or just enjoy a walk anywhere within a kilometer of her safehouse. So long as she accepted that CIA minders would always be accompanying her.

But despite all that, Su felt like she was in prison.

She spent most of her time working inside the secure CIA compound. Only two roads led to the remote ranch complex, one to the north and one to the south. The ranch lay deep inside the Virginian forests. There were no other houses within visible range. Aside from her minders, she never saw another soul outside, not even during her longest walks.

But inside the complex, Su knew she was being watched. CCTV cameras and other electronic sensors watched everything. Armed guards with dogs patrolled the property day and night. They obviously believed she was a valuable prize to offer her this much protection.

After five grueling days of debriefings by nameless men and women, Su finally learned that Caine and Tyler's mission had been a success. They had crushed El Lobizon and the Tumaco Cartel. Captain Zhao Jianyu had failed to transport any sizable quantity of cocaine onboard his submarine. And NSA SIGINT confirmed the MSS believed Su had been killed in La Paz. They were no longer searching for her.

She was safe now, her new handlers told her. Her slate had been wiped clean. She could start over.

She would be protected by the CIA until the day she died. In time, she would be provided with a new American identity. Assuming there were no security issues they were not yet aware of, she would begin work as a CIA analyst on their China Desk.

But until she was cleared, Su remained a prisoner in the remote government ranch. She worked at a desktop computer with access to restricted CIA severs. She had everything she needed to provide her new government with intel from the PLA Navy's submarine navigation program. Within forty-eight hours, Su had downloaded the movements of all known Chinese submarines. She even provided real time intelligence reports. The encrypted records logged every time a submarine surfaced to send a secure transmission to China's spy satellite network.

So far, everything was progressing better than Su Liao had hoped.

But she couldn't help feeling sad. Depressed, even.

No one here was friendly to her. Her life was devoid of warmth. There was nothing to distract herself with, not even paperback books to read. Only work, exercise, eating and sleeping.

But worse than that, a nagging worry had wormed its way into her thoughts. Her parents... Were they really dead? Or were they still languishing in a prison somewhere, tortured on a daily basis?

Her greatest fear was that she might never know the answer to that question.

On her fifteenth day at the safehouse, Su had a visitor.

Rebecca Freeling.

"How are you holding up?" Rebecca asked as they walked together through the trees. A cloud of vapor expelled from her mouth as she spoke. The air was crisp, and a light snow dusted the cold, hard earth. Both women wore winter coats, mittens and scarfs. Golden rays of morning sunlight streamed through the bare branches of the spruce trees.

"Fine," Su said. Her voice was flat, and she kept her eyes on the ground as she walked.

"It will be difficult to adjust," Rebecca offered. "What you've done... I know it can't be easy. You left your old life behind. And there's no going back."

Su nodded and brushed her hair behind her ear. She kept walking. Movement was the only activity that stopped her from screaming at the top of her lungs.

"The intel you are providing us is top rate," Rebecca offered, rubbing her hands together to warm them. "You should be proud."

"Proud? I've betrayed my country," Su responded in a morose whisper.

"They betrayed you." Rebecca's voice was firm but kind. "You had no choice."

"I could have chosen death."

Rebecca shook her head. "That is never a choice you should have to make for yourself." She stopped in her tracks, and took Su's hands in hers. They turned to face each other. "You had an impossible choice, Su. You have to understand that. This hasn't been easy, and

I'm not promising it ever will be. But you had no choice. We were, and still are, your best option."

Su nodded and looked away. Her eyes were damp, and her lower lip quivered. She held her breath, forcing herself not to cry. She didn't want Rebecca to see how much pain she was in.

"Will I see Mr. Caine again?" she finally asked. She felt indebted to him. She knew he had a dark side, but he had shown her kindness. Maybe he could convince her she had made the right choice. And more importantly, he might be the only person who could honestly determine, one way or the other, the fate of her parents.

Rebecca shook her head. "It doesn't work like that. There is no operational reason why you two will ever need to meet again. You need to forget about him."

"Is that what you tell yourself?" Su asked. Her words came out as a harsh whisper.

Rebecca squinted at her, exhaling another puff of mist between them.

"I saw the way you looked at him. You're in love with him, Ms. Freeling." Su continued. "But something is holding you back."

"My relationship with Tom is none of your business."

Su stuffed her hands in her pockets, and resumed walking along the sun-dappled path. Rebecca was the one person she considered to be anything close to a friend here. The last thing she wanted to do was offend her. She quickly changed the subject. "I can't sleep. I can't eat. I'm worried sick about my parents."

Rebecca nodded. "I'm sorry, Su. I know it must be hard."

"Is there any way you can find out...?" Su felt her words stick in her throat. She choked back a sob. "Is there... if they are alive?"

"Is there any chance of getting them out of China?" Rebecca asked, kindness in her words again.

Su burst into tears. She had been holding so many emotions in check for so long, and now she felt she had no will left.

Rebecca wrapped her in a warm embrace. Su's body trembled and shook in her arms. Finally, her crying faded to a muted whimper as Rebecca hugged Su tight. Rebecca's sudden affection comforted her, but she wasn't used to it. She didn't know if she deserved to feel better. Not when her parents might be suffering...

"I can't promise anything," Rebecca said quietly. "But I'll look into..." Rebecca didn't finish her sentence. She hugged Su tighter.

Eventually, Su pulled away. They continued wandering through the pale white hills in silence, each lost in their thoughts.

Rebecca met with Jezebel Yan in a diner on Highway 220. Apart from a surly waitress and a pair of truckers eating eggs, the two women were the only other patrons. Outside the grease-stained windows, the rolling green hills were spotted with patches of snow. Row after row of cedar pines reached up into the brilliant blue sky. Rebecca sighed. This was the kind of place she would enjoy retiring to in her later years.

Yan sipped from a tall glass of orange juice. When Rebecca sat down, the waitress approached and offered them both coffee. Each drank theirs black. Yan sweetened hers with several teaspoons of sugar.

"So? How is she doing?" Yan asked in a matter-of-fact voice.

"So far, everything looks positive," Rebecca said, adding a shrug. "Su's scared, of course. It's been a shock for her, adjusting. But at the end of the day, I think she's the real deal."

Yan nodded, looking somewhat relieved. It had been her reputation on the line as much as Rebecca's. She took a sip of coffee, and peered over the rim of her glasses. "You do know she's hacked into the Internet? Visited many websites outside her mandate?"

"Yes. She's looking for information about her parents..."

Yan lowered her eyes. "What about them?"

Rebecca stared at her across the table. "Look, I haven't said anything. But you and I both know Su's parents are alive. They're imprisoned in a reeducation camp in Xinjiang. Not far from the border with Kyrgyzstan."

"If you tell her that," Yan snapped, "it will destroy her. Then we will lose her, and her intel. And you know we haven't had an intelligence coup like this for years."

Rebecca looked out the window. She watched as a semi-trailer truck thundered past outside, disturbing the peaceful morning. "I know, Jezebel, I know. But I've been thinking. What if we could get them out? It would make a world of difference to Su. Motivate her to help us even more. Plus, it eliminates any risk of Su defecting back to China."

Yan finished her coffee and looked away also. Rebecca recognized the distant look on the woman's face. She had felt the same way after she left Su Liao. They both knew they were destroying this woman's soul. *But that's the way this game is played*, Rebecca mused. Recruit the talent, then suck them dry, until they could no longer deliver. Su Liao would be no different.

"You've got a week off," Yan said, changing the subject. "Hawaii, right?"

Rebecca nodded. She had mixed feelings about that. It bothered her that Su had guessed right about her feelings towards Tom. She hated that her personal life was so obvious to others. Especially an asset like Su…

"You need a break, Rebecca," Yan continued. "Go and enjoy yourself. Refresh. When you come back, who knows…"

Rebecca nodded and forced herself to smile.

Yan threw some money on the table. "Coffee's on me. I'll see you in a week." She stood and walked out.

Rebecca sat with her coffee for a moment. She couldn't help but reflect on her own motivations in all of this. How much did she really care about Tom? How important was her career at the CIA? How many compromises would she make to get what she wanted, despite the cost to others?

Yan was right. Rebecca needed distance and downtime if she was ever to get any real clarity on how she felt. A week lying on the beach with Tom at her side sounded like bliss.

Another truck rumbled by, shaking her from her thoughts. She finished her coffee, then stepped outside into the beautiful Virginia morning.

CHAPTER TWENTY-FOUR

MAUI, HAWAII, UNITED STATES

Caine watched Rebecca saunter out of the lapping ocean waves, and step onto the pristine white sand. Her black bikini left little to the imagination. Her hips swayed from side to side as she walked towards him. Smiling happily, she ran her hands through her wet copper-colored hair. Rivulets of water ran across her chest and down her flat, toned belly. When she reached Caine, she gave him a quick kiss. Then she stretched out on the towel next to his and closed her eyes.

Life, Caine mused, had never been better.

"I know you're watching me," Rebecca said as she slipped on her sunglasses."

"I don't want to look at anything else."

He wore a pair of navy blue board shorts. His legs were marked with a few bruises, most of which had faded to dull, yellow and orange splotches. The blows from Supay's hammer were still angry purple welts, and a scar ran along his arm from the knife attack. Rebecca's tan body was unblemished and perfect.

"What's on your mind, Tom?" she asked, her voice slow and languid.

"I'm thinking how beautiful you are."

She smiled. He could tell she enjoyed the compliment.

While she rested he sat on his beach towel and looked out across the water. The sun hung over the Pacific Ocean, bathing them in its warm rays. In a few hours, the blazing orb would fall beneath the horizon, painting the sky in brilliant streaks of purple and orange.

"A whole week of this," he said with a grin. "I could get used to it."

"It's only our first day. Let's not rush anything."

"I have no intention to."

He leaned in and kissed her.

Her mouth met his. Her hands wrapped around his neck and pulled him close. Soon their bodies were intertwined. Caine felt himself losing control. He wanted Rebecca like he had never wanted anything else in his life.

Fifteen minutes later Caine had Rebecca inside their luxury resort room, standing before their king-sized bed. The view from the floor to ceiling window looked out over the ocean, and the mountainous island of Kaho'olawe.

Their hands tore at each other's clothes. Her beach shirt went up over her head. He pulled at the strings of her bikini, and the tiny scraps of fabric fell away. She tugged at his board shorts as he pulled her onto the bed, devouring her body with his rough kisses. She moaned with pleasure.

They made love until the sun was gone, and the black water outside shimmered in the moonlight

---

Later, Caine leaned against the bed's padded headboard. He stared out the window at the dark waves breaking on the beach. Rebecca lay face down next to him, the sheets puddled around her legs. Caine's hand traced a path across her bare skin, caressing from her shoulder to her thigh and back again. Outside, they could hear the ocean murmur, and insects buzzing in the tropical air. The sounds had a calming effect on them both.

"The website didn't lie... This is paradise," Rebecca purred.

"I've never taken a vacation like this," he said, as his fingers circled the small of her back. "I never understood the appeal of resorts until now."

Rebecca moaned in agreement. For a while, they both settled into a long, very comfortable silence.

The chirp of her cell phone broke the tranquility.

Caine almost asked her not to take it. But in their occupation, he knew that was not an option.

She groaned, and rolled out of the bed. She stretched her arms as she padded over to the phone on the table.

"Hello?" she said. She listened for a second, then rattled off a series of code words. "Oregon, Uniform, Alpha, seven eight, three five, Juliet, seven."

The conversation continued for several minutes. Rebecca made a series of affirmative noises, nodded her head as she listened. Caine found it strangely alluring, watching her be briefed by a faceless bureaucrat on the other side of the world, as she stood naked before him. But his arousal was tempered by the fact that the longer the call lasted, the more likely their time together would come to a sudden end.

Five minutes later Rebecca ended the call. She came to Caine, and straddled him in the bed. Her finger traced a line around the bruise on his forearm, the mark left by Supay's hammer.

She kissed him, gently at first. Then the touch of her lips grew hungry, passionate. But she broke it off a few seconds later, and leaned away from him. "Thank you for doing this, Tom. This was wonderful."

"You have to go?"

She nodded. "I'm sorry. I told you this might happen."

Caine sighed. He could have complained, but what was the point? They were both professionals. The situation was what it was, and nothing he could say or do would change it. But that didn't do anything to lessen his disappointment. "When do you need to leave?"

"I have to go right away." She climbed off him. She gathered her clothes off the floor and started dressing.

Caine climbed out of the bed and pulled on his light cotton pants. "Want me to drive you to the airport?"

She shook her head, and kissed him again. "Why don't you stay? No point both of us missing out on all of this." When she pulled away, the hairs on the back of his neck tingled. The look in her eyes... It was fear. She was afraid of something, even though she was doing her best to mask it.

"Are you okay?" he asked.

"I'm fine." He knew she was lying, but he wasn't sure why. There was a lot about their work they could never share with each other. He kept secrets from her. He assumed she had to do the same, from time to time. "I'll tell you what... When I get back, why don't you break out those Police and Talking Heads albums you keep telling me I should listen to?"

Caine nodded. PT was code for Portugal. That was a relatively safe country. He would worry less knowing she was in Europe and not some hellhole in Africa or the Middle East. And if she got into trouble, it would be an easy country for him to reach and find his way to her again. "Sure. Sounds great."

She buttoned her blouse, then pulled her fiery hair into a ponytail. Her travel bag was already packed, as was his... Standard practice for operatives who might need to leave a location at a moment's notice.

She kissed him a final time. "I'm sorry, Tom. Honestly, stay and enjoy yourself."

She went to leave but he pulled her close one last time. "Be careful," he whispered.

She smiled, but there was something sad in her expression. "I'll be fine. Don't worry about me, this is just routine analyst work."

Then she was gone. Caine was alone in the hotel room.

After a minute, he went to his luggage and found the gift box he had hidden there before flying out. He slid the box open. A set of freshly cut keys lay inside. They glinted in the dim light.

He closed the box, and stuffed it back into his bag. He stood at the window, and watched the ocean creep farther up the pale stretch of sand.

The keys in the box were for his apartment. Rebecca had left before he had a chance to give them to her. Before he told her what he wanted for them, for their future.

He was ashamed to admit it, but he felt relieved.

CHAPTER TWENTY-FIVE

KASHGAR, XINJIANG, CHINA

"I don't like it," Jack Tyler muttered. His body was frozen in place, and only his lips moved. He peered down the scope of a Chinese QBU-88 sniper rifle. His target was an isolated stretch of bitumen road in the mountains. The road led north, out of the city of Kashgar and into the Tian Shan range. Traffic was sparse. Only the occasional battered old truck or rusting car puttered across the rifle's sites.

Rebecca Freeling acted as Tyler's spotter. She read each vehicle's license plate numbers through her binoculars. The jagged, mountainous terrain surrounding them was desolate and bleak. The temperature was well below freezing, chilling her bones even through her thick coat.

The road below was empty and still. Rebecca checked her watch. It was five in the afternoon, Beijing time. There were at least three more hours of daylight. With any luck the prisoner transport would show before nightfall. That would give them just enough time to disappear into the dark mountains. A waiting helicopter would airlift them back to Masas Air Base, a U.S. Air Force controlled facility in

Kyrgyzstan. Their infiltration into China was only possible here, in this very spot, due to the proximity of the Chinese-Kyrgyzstan border.

"You don't have to like it, Tyler." Rebecca felt the cold air sting her lungs every time she spoke. "You just have to do your job."

Tyler was silent. Rebecca knew she was being short with the former Delta Force operator. He'd complained for hours now, grating on her nerves. But despite that, Jack was a professional. His eyes never once left his scope, and his trigger finger was always ready.

When he said nothing more, Rebecca checked in on the two other SAD Operators in their team. They were stationed in the mountain rise on the opposite side of the road. Both men returned her signal. They were also armed with Chinese-made assault rifles, pistols and equipment. None of them wore or carried anything that could identify them as American military. Their cover was as unofficial as it got. If the Chinese authorities caught any of them, it was game over. No one would come for them. It was for that reason, Rebecca knew, that Tyler grumbled. He didn't think the targets were worth the risk.

"The intelligence is good," Rebecca said in a cool, monotone voice. She wasn't sure who she was really trying to convince... Herself, or Tyler. The longer they waited out here, the more she began to doubt their plan. "Su Liao's parents are being moved. Transfer from the Kashgar reeducation camp to another facility in the mountains."

"And you think we'll win Su Liao's heart and mind if we arrange a little family reunion?" Tyler drawled.

Rebecca focused the binoculars on the road again. "What do you think? Su Liao is the best intelligence asset we've recruited from China in decades. If this makes her more productive, the benefits—"

"She's still a defector, ma'am. If she can betray her own people, what will stop her doing the same—"

"And that's why we grab her parents, Tyler. If we have them, she won't want to run."

They heard a noise. A rigid truck appeared on the road headed north. Rebecca read the number plate. She sighed in disappointment. "Wrong truck," she muttered.

Their intelligence had come from the NSA, about two days ago. A hack of a cell phone signal, sourced from within the Kashgar reeducation camp. It gave them a time and a route. Someone in the MSS had concluded that Captain Zhao Jianyu had been responsible for placing Su's parents in custody. Whoever it was, they had ordered that the elderly couple be transferred.

"That's a negative," Rebecca said into her radio. Corporals Jefferson Huang and Peter Kalkan on the opposite mountain rise answered back. "Copy that. All teams, remain in overwatch."

"Well that's a letdown," Tyler grumbled again. "I could do with some action. I'd say my ass is getting sore for sitting around all day. But it's not my ass that has a problem. It being pointed upwards and all."

Rebecca turned her head to hide her smile. Tyler's joking did have a calming effect on her, despite his stubborn attitude. "Caine said you never stopped talking."

"Is that right?" Tyler chuckled without moving. "That's because Tom's got the personality of a spare tire. I had to fill a lot of uncomfortable silences back in La Paz."

Rebecca chuckled. "Sounds like you two are made for each other."

Tyler was quiet for a moment. Then he spoke up again. "Ma'am, it's no secret that you two... well, you know what I mean. So why didn't you bring him along?"

Inside Rebecca cringed. Despite her reservations, she knew she was falling for Caine more and more each day. That was exactly why she had not brought him along. And that was why she had lied to him about where she was going.

"Caine's compromised," she replied. "If one of us gets caught, we can at least hope for a prisoner exchange. But Tom—the MSS will execute him on the spot."

"You underestimate him," Tyler said, his voice a low growl. "He's rough around the edges but—"

"Like I said, you're perfect for each other."

Tyler chuckled. "All I'm saying is, if there is one man I want covering my back, it's Caine. Present company excluded, of course."

"I think I resent that remark, Tyler." Rebecca turned her attention back to the road. A bicycle overloaded with many sacks of grain worked its way south. There was no need to call this one in.

"Anyway, things with Tom and me... It's complicated," Rebecca felt compelled to say.

"Yeah," Tyler muttered. "It always is."

She heard another truck, rumbling in the distance. This one was moving fast, powering up the mountain road, and leaving a trail of dust trail in its wake. Rebecca struggled to focus her binoculars on its mud spattered license plates.

CRACK! CRACK!

Gunfire rang out. Two shoots, one after the other, echoed through the mountains.

"All units, who the hell is shooting?" Rebecca hissed into her radio.

Before anyone could answer, another shot rang out from nearby. Tyler swore, and she saw sparks flash from his rifle. He dropped the gun and shuffled back in the dirt. It had been shot out of his hands.

They both rolled onto their back, drawing pistols to engage whoever it was who had snuck up behind them.

But there was no point.

A dozen PLA soldiers swept through the snow covered rocks. Within seconds, the soldiers had the pair lined up in the sights of their QBZ-95 Assault Rifles. Tyler put a hand on Rebecca's shoulder. He looked her in the eyes and shook his head. She knew what he was trying to tell her. There was no way the soldiers could miss at this range. They dropped their pistols on the cold, hard ground.

One of the soldiers stepped forward, and retrieved their weapons. Another man emerged from the shadows of a rock outcropping. He wore an expensive parka and khaki pants, and his desert boots were clean and unmarked. He pulled down his hood, revealing slicked back hair, parted carefully on the left.

"Rebecca Freeling," Chen Fa Li said, baring his teeth with a wide grin. "So lovely to see you again."

CHAPTER TWENTY-SIX

Rebecca and Tyler were handcuffed, then marched at gunpoint down to the road. Several FAW MV3 military transportation trucks pulled up, delivering even more soldiers. Rebecca's heart sank. Huang and Kalkan's corpses tumbled down the hill on the opposite side. Their blood left a crimson smear across the snow and rocks.

They knew we were coming, Rebecca realized. This mission was compromised from the start.

A canvas bag was pulled over her head. Rebecca felt herself being shoved into the back of one of the trucks. She winced as she banged her head on the rear door. Despite the pain, she felt strangely optimistic. If they hadn't killed her and Tyler already, she figured they still needed them for some reason. If she was of value, she might still be able to negotiate their release. It was the only hope she could still hang on to.

The truck drove for an hour or more, headed deeper into the mountains. Trapped in darkness, she could feel the truck shimmy and groan, as the winding road became steeper. She tried to sense if Tyler was nearby. It was impossible to be sure, but she suspected he was on one of the other trucks.

When they finally stopped, Rebecca felt several hands pull her from the truck. She stumbled as they dragged her across the frozen earth. They entered a building of some kind. She passed through many doors. Suddenly, the bag was snatched from her head. As she blinked in the blinding interior lights, soldiers removed her cuffs.

Her vision came into focus. The three soldiers in the room were female. Their expressions were hard and cruel, devoid of any other emotions.

"Strip!" the older woman shouted in Mandarin. Her hair was pinned in a tight bun, and it was starting to grey. A few wrinkles lined her eyes and lips.

"What?" Rebecca asked, not sure she had heard the woman correctly.

The woman lashed out with a bamboo stick, striking Rebecca on the face. Rebecca recoiled, more from the shock. Then she felt the red hot pain of a welt across her cheek. She touched her skin and her hand came away sticky with blood.

"Strip!" said the woman again, threatening with the stick.

Within a minute Rebecca was standing naked in the cold room. She covered her chest with her arms, and shivered.

The woman struck her again, this time across the back. She pointed to a concrete wall.

Rebecca didn't want to think about what was coming. It couldn't be good. She tried to remember her training. Be observant. Look for anything, no matter how small, that could be used to her advantage. But she saw nothing.

The woman struck Rebecca several more times, drawing welts and blood. She kept motioning with the bamboo stick until Rebecca finally comprehended that she had to stand tall, with her back straight and arms by her side. Only when Rebecca was motionless did the beating stop. But she couldn't stop shaking.

Two male soldiers entered, dragging a long fire hose behind them. They turned up the pressure, then blasted her with cold water. Soon Rebecca was forced up against the concrete wall. The icy spray felt like needles, stabbing at her skin. Each time she fell to the ground, the woman hit her with the bamboo until she stood tall again. She sobbed, and begged for the ordeal to end.

After what seemed like hours the hosing and beating ceased. Her hands were again cuffed. She was taken by the female soldiers to a dark cell that smelled of mold and sewage. The women cuffed her to a metal chair, then left the room.

Rebecca looked down at her bare legs and arms. They were covered in bruises from the force of the water cannon. Her welts were raw and purple, seeping blood across her skin.

As bad as it was, Rebecca knew things could have been worse. Much worse.

Rebecca had read the after-action reports from Colombia. She knew Tyler and Caine had been tortured there. Neither man had talked about what had happened afterwards. But now she had been tortured for the first time in her life. Those reports haunted her. It wasn't academic, what the men had experienced. It was real. It was a nightmare. Rebecca was like them now. How could Tom not have shared with her how horrible his ordeal had been? How was he able to bottle it all up inside?

Hours later, another man entered the room. He stood in the shadows for a moment, a silhouette against the light spilling in from the corridor outside. He stood there for what felt like several minutes, staring at her naked body. Watching her shiver.

Rebecca turned her head. A curl of fiery hair fell across her face. She glared up at the shadow in the door. "Enjoying yourself?" she snapped.

The man stepped closer, moving into the light.

She recognized him at once. It was Chen Fa Li. The MSS operative from Hong Kong. The man who had allowed Caine to leave Hong Kong unhindered. At the time, she had wondered why.

He took several photos of her with a digital camera. He grabbed her chin and forced her head up as he snapped more pictures of her face. He obviously wanted to make sure she was recognized.

When he finished, he pulled another metal chair from against the wall and sat next to her. "Rebecca Freeling," he said in perfect English. "I must offer you my apologies. I regret that I had to put you through all that."

"No," Rebecca snarled. "I don't think you do. You're a sadist, and a pig."

"I was born in the Year of the Pig," he said, amused. "This is not an insult in China. We pigs have great concentration. Once we set a goal for ourselves, we devote all energy to achieving it. That is exactly what I am doing here."

"Is that so? Because it looks to me like all you're doing is getting yourself off."

Chen grinned. "Have no fear Ms. Freeling, this has all been for a calculated effect. You will not be tortured again. At least not until I get what I want. If everything goes as planned, you and your friend, Mr. Tyler, will soon return to your homeland."

Rebecca's eyes blazed with fury. "And what about Huang and Kalkan?"

Chen looked away, as if to consider his next words before speaking them. "There is no point lying to you. Those two men had no emotional connection to Caine. There was no reason to keep them alive."

Rebecca frowned. "If you think I'll help you lay a trap for Tom, you are very much mistaken."

Chen laughed. "Oh, that is most amusing, Ms. Freeling. You see, I don't need your help to lay a trap. The trap is already set. Now, I just need to convince Mr. Caine that if he doesn't do exactly what I ask of him, then you and Tyler will be executed. I think these photos will prove to be quite convincing, don't you think?"

Chen clicked his fingers. The two younger female soldiers returned to the room. One carried a cup of hot tea. The other a bundle of clothes.

Chen took a key from his pocket. He tapped it against his palm, then used it to uncuff Rebecca from the chair. He took the tea from the first woman and handed it to Rebecca. "Drink," he said, despite her suspicious stare. "It is jasmine tea. It will warm you. Please, relax. There are far faster and easier ways to kill you than poisoning."

Rebecca took the tea and drank quickly. When she was done the woman handed her the clothing, a pair of utilitarian blue prison scrubs. Rebecca dressed fast. The warmth was a welcome relief, but the pain of her beatings was no longer dulled by the cold.

Chen offered her more tea. Rebecca accepted. Its warmth surged through her tired body, reviving her strength, giving her hope.

"So what happens now?" she asked.

"Nothing," Chen answered, adding a bemused smile. "You are our guest here. You shall be treated fairly. When I return, I am quite sure Mr. Caine will have done what I ask of him. In which case you and Tyler will be released back to America."

"And if he doesn't?" Rebecca asked. She already knew the answer to her question.

He smiled. "I don't think we need to talk about the unpleasantries of life, and death, any further, do we Ms. Freeling? Now... let us enjoy some more of this delicious tea."

CHAPTER TWENTY-SEVEN

MAUI, HAWAII, UNITED STATES

Caine's feet pounded across the damp earth. Sweat drenched his body, and his thin t-shirt clung to his skin. His breathing was rapid and labored. He knew he was pushing himself, but it took extreme discipline to keep his lean and muscular body in top physical shape. For the last four mornings in a row, he woke at dawn to exercise. He ran along a path through the subtropical forests, up the side of Maui's largest peak. He figured this morning he'd increase his sprint elevation by another thousand feet. Push himself even further.

After Rebecca's sudden departure Caine had considered cutting his trip short. Then he'd figured, when was the last time he had taken a vacation? Years? Never? There was nothing urgent waiting for him back at Langley. And there was always the possibility Rebecca's assignment would end early. Perhaps she could fly back, and they could spend a last day or two together.

Caine pushed the whimsical thoughts from his mind and sprinted up the next stretch. The tropical scrub grew close to the path here. Caine's senses sharpened, he became more alert. In the field, this would have been the perfect location for an ambush.

As he rounded a bend in the path, he spotted a figure up ahead. An Asian man stepped out of the dense foliage, and stood waiting under a grove of palm trees.

Caine froze in his tracks. He recognized Chen Fa Li immediately.

A smug grin was plastered across The Ministry of State Security officer's face. The man ran a hand over his slick hair, ensuring the left side part remained in place. He wore light blue cotton pants, sneakers and a Hawaiian shirt. The outfit matched the attire of the many tourists on the island. Caine walked closer, taking a good look at the man's clothes. He didn't spot any telltale bulges of concealed weapons on Chen's body, but it was impossible to be sure.

"Mr. Caine," Chen said pleasantly. "What a surprise."

"I doubt that." Caine scanned the surroundings. The scrub grew dense and close on all sides. There could be armed men hidden in the foliage less than a hundred feet away and he wouldn't be able to see them. "I'm assuming you didn't come alone?"

"That would be a wise assumption." Chen carefully reached into his pants pocket and withdrew a cell phone. "I only want to talk, and show you something."

Caine's sensors were on overdrive. He tensed, ready to spring into action, take down the other operatives Chen had brought with him. But some rational corner of Caine's mind argued against that course of action.

If he wanted to kill me, he could have already taken a shot, he thought.

"How did you know I was here?" Caine asked. "I flew in under an assumed identity."

Chen laughed. "I'm MSS. Do not underestimate our capabilities. You were easy enough to find."

"So what is it you want?"

"To show you some photographs, Caine." He passed over the cell phone.

Caine glanced down at the phone. The photo on the screen showed Rebecca Freeling, handcuffed and bound naked to a chair in a dark cell. Her skin was bruised and beaten.

Caine clenched his jaw as he flipped through the photographs. More of the same. She had been tortured, there was no doubt about that. He flipped again, coming across similar photos of Jack Tyler.

Caine's face flushed with anger. He clenched the phone in a white-knuckle grip, and stalked towards Chen. "Where are they, Chen?" he snarled. "I don't care how many men you have in the trees... they won't be able to stop me before I tear out your throat."

Chen took a few steps back. "Don't be so hasty, Mr. Caine. If you want them to live, you must listen to what I say."

The foliage around them rustled. Several armed Chinese men emerged from the undergrowth. Each carried a semi-automatic pistol, which they aimed carefully at Caine.

Caine glared at Chen. He clenched and unclenched his fists as he panted for breath.

"Relax, Mr. Caine," Chen said. He smoothed out the creases in his clothes. "Tyler and Freeling are both fine for the moment. You can have them back, mostly intact, after you do a job for me."

Caine focused on controlling his breathing. He kept his eyes fixed on the man before him, ignoring the others. "What kind of job?" he asked.

"You are an assassin, are you not?"

Caine didn't answer. His emerald eyes grew dark as he stared down the Chinese operative. He imagined his fingers wrapping around the man's slim neck, and throttling the life out of him.

That's not going to help Rebecca or Jack, he thought. *Got to keep this asshole talking.*

"Why? Who do you want killed?" he asked.

"Captain Zhao Jianyu. The commanding officer, or should I say, former commanding officer, of the nuclear submarine *Hai Long*."

Caine took a moment to consider the request. The Chinese agents fanned out around him, keeping him in their sights.

Caine laughed without humor. "Right. I take it you don't approve of Zhao's little stunt in Columbia?"

Chen smiled again. "As you say. Zhao has gone too far. I would take care of him myself, but the man still has powerful connections in the Communist Party. It would cost me valuable political capital if I issued orders for his arrest and execution. Zhao gave in to capitalist temptations. He used government property to smuggle drugs into America. This unsanctioned activity could have caused an international incident. But still, his connections offer him protection."

Caine kept his expression impassive. He was surprised how much Chen knew about Caine's recent operations in South America. "I heard Zhao was in debt to some nasty criminals. Doesn't sound like much of a threat to me."

"He is a threat to nationalist ideals."

"You mean he is a threat to you," Caine countered.

Chen tilted his head thoughtfully as he considered Caine's words. "I suppose he is. Either way, he must be dealt with, and I cannot be involved. But a rogue American agent with a personal vendetta against Zhao... "

"There is no way I could get close to him, Chen," Caine countered. "Not in Beijing. I'd be arrested the moment I stepped into your country."

"That is the beauty of it. Zhao is not in China. He's been, how shall I put it, 'encouraged' to take a holiday. He's currently in Bali, Indonesia. Ever been there?"

Caine didn't answer.

"I have a ticket waiting for you. You leave tonight. That is, if you want to see Freeling and Tyler alive again."

Caine's fist clenched even tighter. A loud crack echoed through the forest, and Chen jumped slightly, as his men tensed. Caine dropped the remains of the cell phone to the ground. The screen had shattered in his white-knuckled grip.

He stared at Chen, and took a deep breath. "Very well. But if I do this, there's one thing you need to understand."

"And what is that, Mr. Caine?" Chen asked, once again smoothing out the part in his hair.

"If you or your people touch Rebecca and Jack again... Zhao won't be the only one who dies."

Chen smiled, but his eye twitched, and his face looked a bit paler than normal. "Of course Mr. Caine. There is no need for any further unpleasantness."

Caine nodded. "Alright. So what's the plan?"

CHAPTER TWENTY-EIGHT

Within an hour Caine found himself disguised in the grease stained overalls of a flight technician. He carried a fake Russian passport, complete with a recent photograph. The document listed his birthplace as Kazan. Caine couldn't fault the forgery. The work was as good as anything he had seen the CIA produce.

Chen Fa Li and two of his men wore similar outfits. Together they passed through immigration and customs without incident. Then the four men marched to the cargo terminal. Their flight out of Hawaii was on a Shaanxi Y-8 four prop cargo plane. The medium sized aircraft was the Chinese version of the Soviet Antonov An-12. As he walked through the cargo bay, Caine noted the plane was nearly empty. Chen's men led him to the passenger deck, and within minutes they were taxiing down the runway.

He found a seat in the passenger deck and buckled in. No attempts were made to threaten Caine or restrain him. As long as Chen held Rebecca and Jack, the MSS operative knew Caine wasn't going anywhere.

When they were airborne and the seat belt lights were extinguished, Caine got up and stretched. Chen watched with a bemused expression, as Caine paced up and down the aisle of the plane.

"You should rest Caine. It's ten thousand kilometers to Bali, with a stopover in Micronesia to refuel."

Caine turned and stared Chen down. His raging eyes felt like dark knives aimed at Chen's heart. "How about you use the time to finish briefing me on your plan. How is this going to work?"

"Of course. As I told you before, our flight is logged for Jakarta via Pohnpei. Once you are in Bali you will—"

"If we're landing in Jakarta, how exactly am I supposed to get into Bali?" Caine asked, cutting him off.

Chen smiled. "Simple, Mr. Caine. As we pass over Bali you will perform a high altitude low opening jump—"

"A HALO jump?" Caine gave the man an incredulous stare. "You're insane."

Chen removed a bottle of whiskey from under his seat. He poured himself a glass. "I don't know through which special forces outfit you received your training. That is a highly guarded secret. But I do know you have logged over a hundred HALO jumps."

Caine wished Chen's intelligence was wrong, but it wasn't.

Chen took a sip of the amber scotch, then licked his lips. "You will freefall most of the way to avoid radar detection. No one will know you have entered the country. We don't have to deviate from our flight path, so my people and I will have sufficient deniability." He finished his whiskey and poured another glass. He held it out to Caine.

Caine shook his head. If Chen meant what he said about a HALO jump, Caine knew he would have to keep his head clear, his reflexes sharp.

Chen shrugged, and sipped from the glass himself. "Power is always shifting within the Chinese Communist Party. Politics is simply another game. And like any other game, there are winners and there are losers."

"And you want to be one of the winners?"

"I do." Chen grinned again. "Exposing what Zhao did will be beneficial to my standing in the Party, but I can't be seen as the one dealing out justice. I will be perceived as, how do I say, spiteful? It is better if he disappears, before I present my case."

"So he won't be around to contradict you?"

Chen gave another of his smug grins. Caine resisted the urge to punch him in the face. "Yes, Mr. Caine. You are better at this game than I thought. Which reminds me, there is another matter we must discuss. I am speaking of Su Liao, of course.

Caine kept his face cold and devoid of emotion. "There's nothing to discuss. She's dead, Chen. The Colombians got to her, right after they took out your operatives in La Paz."

This time Chen laughed sincerely. "Perhaps I praised your skill too soon. I do enjoy watching people when they lie. I know Su Liao is very much alive and well. She is living in America, helping you hack into the PLA Navy's submarine tracking system."

Without consciously being aware of his actions, Caine tensed and curled his hands into fists.

Of course, he thought. *Chen had access to Rebecca and Jack for days... he must have pumped them for intel when he had them beaten and tortured. No one can hold out forever...*

If Chen noticed Caine's simmering rage, he said nothing. He took another sip of whiskey. "That vulnerability will be eliminated soon enough. Su Liao will be useless to you in a matter of days. But what she did reveal could potentially be embarrassing for China if it got out. And I was the agent responsible for monitoring her at the time."

"Another reason to get rid of Zhao. He links you to Su Liao."

"Yes, indeed. Therefore, I am willing to make one more deal with you, to ensure this operation proceeds smoothly."

"Which is?" Caine asked, his interest piqued.

"Not only will I return Freeling and Tyler, but I'll give you Liao's parents as well."

Caine narrowed his eyes. "They're alive?"

"Of course. Ms. Freeling and Mr. Tyler entered my country with the foolish intent of rescuing them. Their plan was idiotic, but it made them the perfect bait."

"I don't get it, Chen. Assuming Su Liao is alive, holding her parents gives you leverage over her."

"Yes, but as I said, she will be useless to both of us soon. China does not wish to be embarrassed by this defection. And we have no easy means by which to find and assassinate her. Pacifying her is the next best option."

Caine's mind ran through all the possible deceptions Chen was scheming here. He didn't trust the man in the slightest. But the chance to secure Liao's parents was too good an opportunity to pass up.

Chen took another sip of whiskey and sighed. "It's not that complicated. I'm not a monster, Mr. Caine. I simply wish to raise my position in the Party. If Su has her parents returned to her, she can focus on a positive future in the United States. I would prefer that, rather than have her use her talents to expose and embarrass me in the future."

Caine rubbed his eyes. He realized he did need some sleep before his jump. He needed to be at the peak of his abilities. A HALO jump came with many risks.

"You see, we can all win here," Chen continued. "You get your friends back. Liao is reunited with her family. And I increase my power and status back home. Plus, you and I have established a working relationship now. That will work for you as much as it will work for me in the future. I will be someone you can reach out to when you want to negotiate with the MSS."

Caine didn't like Chen's proposal. Something was off about it. But it was a better offer than he had expected. And in the end, what choice did he have? He decided he would see the assassination through, even though he was expecting a trap.

"Okay, Chen. You have a deal. But I have one more condition. And it's non-negotiable."

"Oh? And what would that be?" Chen asked, amused.

Caine sat down across from the man, and leaned back as far as his chair would allow. He closed his eyes. "If we ever cross paths again, I will kill you on sight."

CHAPTER TWENTY-NINE

BALI, INDONESIA

As dawn painted the sky in streaks of purple and orange, Caine balanced on the edge of the cargo ramp. The rushing wind buffeted his body, and drowned out the roar of the plane's four engines. He stood motionless for a moment, peering through the clouds at the dark oblivion below. At thirty-five thousand feet, the ocean was a distant, flat gray slate, dotted with tiny curls of white. It looked still and motionless, as if frozen in time. The sight of it was calming somehow. Peaceful.

Caine checked his altimeter and oxygen gauge one last time, making sure everything was working properly. Then he took a deep breath, and stepped off the ramp, plunging into the wind and clouds.

He fell fast. Within seconds he hit terminal velocity. Air resistance slowed the acceleration of his fall to a constant rate. He tumbled around once, watching the Shaanxi Y-8 cargo plane grow small in in the sky as it powered west. He spun again, facing back towards the distant water. He spread his limbs, creating a cross with his body to control his descent. The wind noise was deafening, as he plummeted at one hundred and thirty miles per hour. He checked his altimeter.

Twenty-nine thousand feet... The height of Mount Everest.

The high-altitude air was bitter cold, at a chilling minus forty degrees Fahrenheit. Goggles and gloves protected his extremities from frostbite. His oxygen mask ensured he didn't pass out from hypoxia. He pulled his arms and legs in close, dropping like an arrow towards the warmer air closer to the earth.

At twenty-thousand feet he hit a thick layer of clouds. Everything turned white and the sensation of falling vanished. Caine swallowed hard. He'd always found clouds disconcerting whenever he parachuted. Once inside their hazy white void, he lost all sense of distance or direction. He checked his altimeter again.

Eighteen-thousand feet.

He broke through the clouds. The islands of Bali and Lombok loomed in the brilliant azure sea. Their twin jungle-clad volcanic peaks were cast in long shadows from the morning sun. Caine fell towards the churning sea between them. Known as the Badung Strait, the large body of water lay between Bali and the smaller island of Nusa Penida.

At ten-thousand feet he was as high as the volcanic peaks. The air was warmer now. He could make out roads and clustered urban areas on the islands. It would be about now that nitrogen would bubble out of his blood stream. The sudden change in altitude could cause decompression sickness, like a diver afflicted by the bends. Luckily he had been breathing pure oxygen for the last forty-five minutes. The process had already purged the excess nitrogen from his blood.

At three-thousand feet his parachute snapped open. The process was automatic, although he kept his hand on the ripcord just in case. He felt his body jolt upwards, and his descent slowed. The chute had caught.

He gazed towards the smaller island of Nusa Penida, Zhao's holiday destination. The Chinese submarine captain would be diving at a reef on the western side of the island. Caine had the GPS coordinates. The spot was a five mile swim west from his landing zone. Chen could have dropped Caine closer, but that increased the chances of him being spotted.

A night insertion had also been out of the question. That would have required altering the cargo plane's flight path, drawing unwanted attention from others. Complicating matters, Royal Australian Air Force P-3 Orion spy planes frequented the area. Caine didn't want to attract their interest with his insertion any more than Chen did. The Shaanxi cargo plane pilots had pushed their flight schedule as it was to get here by dawn.

As the ocean waves raced towards him Caine disconnected his parachute. He dropped fifteen feet and hit the waves with a quiet splash. He sank deep into the warm tropical waters. Visibility was good; he could see at least eighty feet through the clear blue seawater.

Caine switched from his oxygen tanks to a snorkel. He wore scuba tanks, but he would need them later, after he reached Zhao's yacht. Caine forced himself to breathe slow and steady through the tube, as he paddled just beneath the surface of the water.

He estimated the five mile swim would take between three to five hours, depending on the current. He'd gone similar distances during his special forces training. But those grueling swims had been in cold water without fins or masks, endured after weeks of intense mental and physical training. This would be a day at the beach in comparison.

Caine tugged off his helmet, and replaced it with a diving mask. He removed his gloves and boots, and slipped on a pair of black flippers. Everything he no longer needed was weighed down and sunk. The rest of his equipment was stored in his pack, and attached to his buoyant tactical floatation system.

As he glided through the water, he felt a stinging sensation on his left hand. His skin began to itch and burn. The pain wasn't intense, more of a distraction really. But it slowly began to build.

Within seconds he felt another sting on his right foot. Then one on the back of his neck.

Caine stopped, and hung floating in the water. He swung his head left and right, peering through the depths to identify the source of the irritation.

Then he saw it. A translucent blob, undulating past him in the water. Long, colorful tendrils drifted in the creature's wake. As the strange organism moved past, he saw another ahead of him. Then a dozen. Then hundreds...

A swarm of jellyfish pulsated through the water around him.

A stream of bubbles erupted from Caine's snorkel.

Calm down! His instincts clamped down on his fear and revulsion. *If they were poisonous, you'd already be dead.*

He knew a sting from the lethal box jellyfish species could cause a man to go into cardiac arrest. But the pain from these specimens was manageable, nothing that would slow him down. But there was no clear path through the swarm. They were everywhere. Wherever he looked, hundreds turned into thousands. Thousands became tens of thousands. He was surrounded, trapped in a migrating swarm of the strange, umbrella-shaped marine animals.

He felt their tendrils brush against him, stinging him again and again. His wetsuit protected his torso, along with his arms and legs. But the rest of him was exposed.

He swung his backpack in front of his body, and used it to push jellyfish out of the way. His legs powered him forward with long, slow kicks. He swam east, towards the distant reef and Zhao's yacht. The pack blocked his head and hands from the jellyfish, but the stings on his ankles increased. They felt like a series of electric shocks, each one more powerful than the last.

Caine ignored the pain as best he could and pushed on. Soon the waters were thick with the gelatinous creatures... All he could see were semi-translucent blobs and glistening tentacles. They filled his vision, hovering everywhere in the water.

He swam for what felt like half an hour before the jellyfish swarm dissipated. A few minutes later, they disappeared altogether. Caine was once again alone in the clear blue sea.

He surfaced, using his pack as a flotation device. Catching his breath, he rested for a minute. Then he pulled away the torn tentacles that still adhered to his skin. Treading water, he removed a first aid kit from his pack, and took out the antihistamine tablets. He popped two, and sipped some water from a bottle. Rubbing vinegar into the wounds would relieve the pain, but that was impossible while submerged. He'd just have to live with it.

After resting for fifteen minutes, the pain began to dull. It didn't go away, but he did feel more capable of achieving his mission. Rebecca and Tyler were depending on him. If he did not survive to complete his objective, they would die also. That was a greater motivation than anything else to keep going.

Caine checked his location on his GPS device. He had covered a mile already. When he looked east, he could just make out the peaks of Nusa Penida island.

Gritting his teeth, Caine replaced his goggles and snorkel. He resumed crawling through the shimmering water.

Only four more miles to go.

CHAPTER THIRTY

It was late morning by the time Caine reached Zhao's luxury forty-foot cruising yacht. The vessel lay anchored above a reef about five-hundred feet off the shores of Nusa Penida. In the distance, tropical forests rose up behind the white cliffs and jagged rocks of the island's coast. The water was pristine, and Caine could see the hull of the boat clearly, bobbing with the gentle motion of the sea.

Caine switched to his scuba tanks, deflated his floating tactical bag until it had neutral buoyancy. Then he dove deep, and made his way towards the boat.

As he skimmed the sea floor, the underwater world exploded with color. Thousands of tropical fish and sponges clustered around a vast coral reef. A gigantic mola mola sunfish swam lazily in the water. Its pale, flat body was several feet taller than Caine. He was impressed with the creature's size, estimating the white scaled fish was about four times his body weight.

But as large as it was, mola mola were harmless. He swam past until he found a sandy section of seabed, not far from the hull of Zhao's yacht. He kept his distance from the boat, making sure the bubbles from his scuba equipment would not alert anyone on the surface. He wished Chen had provided him with a rebreather system. That would have eliminated any telltale sign of his presence underwater.

Kneeling in the seabed, Caine collected several watertight pouches from his pack. They contained his SIG Sauer P226 9mm pistol, a speargun and three charged explosives with remote detonation switches. A fighting knife was already strapped to his right leg.

His gear ready, Caine swam to decompression depth and waited. He hovered in the water for several minutes, allowing time for nitrogen bubbles to safely escape his blood. Then he surfaced, making as little noise as possible.

The yacht was only a couple of hundred feet away. A man was working up on the deck. Caine used his optic lens to zoom in, confirming the figure was Zhao. The muscular Chinese sailor wore only shorts. His skin was tan, and his face looked a bit sunburned. He was busy gutting a fish with a long knife.

His target confirmed, Caine dove again. He swam beneath the yacht, coming up next to the bow, where Zhao would be less likely to see him. Working quickly, Caine had placed the three magnetic charges along the length of the hull. When they detonated they would consume the boat, and Zhao along with it.

Satisfied, Caine armed the charges and swam towards the shore.

Several hundred feet from the yacht, Caine surfaced again. He peered through his optic lens, watching to make sure Zhao had not been alerted.

As he focused the lens on the boat, Caine froze in the water.

Three more people had joined Zhao on the deck. A slim Asian woman in her later thirties in a red bikini approached Zhao, embracing him from behind. Two young girls, both no more than ten years old, followed her across the deck.

Caine swore under his breath. Zhao had a family, and he had brought them with him on his holiday. Chen had conveniently left that detail out.

Caine treaded water as he stared at the woman and children. He knew they were innocent. They probably knew nothing about Zhao's illegal activities, or his rivalry with Chen. They were collateral damage. Pawns sacrificed in a game they didn't even realize was being played around them.

But Chen... He had Rebecca and Jack. If Caine didn't complete this mission, it was they who would be sacrificed.

He closed his eyes, and thought for a moment. He heard the sound of the water, waves rising and falling around him. A warm breeze blew across the surface. It carried the muted sounds of the two girls, laughing and playing on the boat in the distance.

The charges are safer, a cold voice whispered in the back of his mind. *A push of a button, and this is all over. Rebecca and Jack will be safe.*

He glanced at the detonator attached to his belt. It swayed up and down in the water.

He made his decision. As if a switch had been flipped, Caine quickly changed from his scuba equipment back to the snorkel. He dove again, holding his breath as he swam down to his tactical pack. He dropped his tanks, and stuffed the detonator and speargun back in the pack.

He made his way for the surface, rising up at the stern of the boat. Caine crawled on board, timing the sound of his movements with the lapping of the waves against the hull. He slipped off his flippers and left his mask on his forehead. Then he slid his P226 pistol from its pouch.

He crept forward, keeping low against the sidewall of the boat. He could hear Zhao laughing with his children, playfully threatening to smear them with the fish entrails.

It was Zhao's wife who saw Caine first. He was crouched only a few feet away from her, his pistol aimed at a point on her forehead. Caine had studied Zhao's file. He knew the attractive woman's name was Li Li. She sucked in her breath, and froze. Her wide brown eyes stared back at him with a mixture of surprise and terror. She grabbed the nearest girl, and held her tight.

Zhao glanced over at her. *"Tā shì shénme?"* he asked. "What is it?" Then, as if suddenly realizing what was happening, he spun around. He held up the filleting knife in a white-knuckle grip.

"You," Zhao growled. "You were supposed to die in Columbia, Caine."

"Sorry to disappoint you," Caine said. His voice was flat, devoid of all emotion.

Zhao's face was red with fury. "So now you are here to kill me? To murder my wife and children?"

"I came to make a deal," Caine lied.

"A deal?" Zhao seemed surprised.

Caine thought for a second. "Your billion dollar drug deal went south," he finally said. "You pissed off a lot of people. You won't survive long on your own. I'm here to offer you a way out."

Li Li sobbed, trembling where she stood. Caine didn't blame her. Nothing could be more terrifying than knowing your own children were being threatened and there was nothing you could do to stop it.

Zhao was tense. The muscles in his body seemed to pulsate with anger and frustration. But his face remained calm as he spoke. "Really? And how exactly do you propose to do that?"

"Let's talk about it. Just you and me. Send Li Li and your children to shore. They don't have to be involved in this."

Zhao stared at Caine in surprise. He started to speak, but the words seemed to die in his throat. His proud features seemed to sag, and his sun-kissed skin went pale.

He nodded and spoke to his wife in Mandarin. Caine couldn't follow the conversation. He could sense it was tense and full of fear. Caine was fairly certain Li Li and her children didn't speak English. They hadn't understood anything that Caine and Zhao had discussed.

Zhao turned back to Caine. "Can I at least say goodbye?"

Caine nodded. He kept his pistol aimed firmly at Zhao.

Caine said nothing as the man embraced his family. After several minutes of kissing and hugging, tears and sobs, Li Li and the children climbed into a motorized dingy. Zhao forced himself to smile at the children as the tiny boat motored towards the shore.

He turned to face Caine, his face a pale, blank mask.

"Letting my family go... I appreciate that, Caine. You are not at all what I expected. But I was right, wasn't I? You are here to kill me?"

"That was my deal," Caine growled. "Your life for theirs."

Zhao glanced at his family's boat. The buzzing of its motor began to fade in the distance. "Please," he said quietly. "Just let them get a little farther away. So the little ones... So they won't hear the shot."

Caine nodded. "Alright Zhao. I'll give you a minute. One more minute. And after that... you die."

CHAPTER THIRTY-ONE

The two men stood alone on the deck of the forty-foot yacht. They stared at each other, neither daring to break eye contact. The deck bobbed up and down, rocked by the gentle motions of the sea. A tropical breeze kissed the tips of the waves that rippled through the water. But for Caine and Zhao, the tranquil beauty was merely a backdrop for their game of life and death.

"How did you find me?" Zhao asked through gritted teeth.

"Easy," Caine answered, keeping his semi-automatic aimed at Zhao's head. "Chen Fa Li told me."

"Chen? The MSS operative? He sent you to kill me?"

Caine nodded. "We made a deal." He had no desire to elaborate any further.

"He knew, all along?"

"About your cocaine smuggling plans? Of course."

Zhao shook his head. "I underestimated him. I should have let El Lobizon's men take care of him for me."

"Like you tried to do to Su Liao? And her family? You imprisoned an innocent woman's parents, just so you could make a buck."

Zhao laughed. "You think you have all the answers, Caine. But you still don't know the truth about Liao."

Caine's finger tightened on the trigger of his gun. He knew he should shoot Zhao and get it over with. But he hesitated. Zhao had caught his attention.

"Alright, Zhao. Enlighten me.

"Well, for one thing, Su Liao is not her real name. She's not even Han Chinese. Su Liao was born Aynur Sabir, to Uyghur parents."

"What?"

Zhao laughed again. "You and the CIA are pathetic when it comes to infiltrating Chinese intelligence. It's not because you lack the technical skills. It is because you don't understand our culture and our way of life. You miss what is right in front of you."

Caine gestured with his weapon. "Keep talking. What happened to her?"

"Her parents were terrorists. They were captured and executed by the PLA when Aynur Sabir was only five. Perhaps the soldiers who killed her family took pity on the girl. Or maybe they were simply incompetent. Either way, young Sabir disappeared, and escaped her parents' fate. Later, I discovered she was taken in by a Han couple who couldn't have children of their own. The Liao family. They brought her up as Han Chinese."

Caine glowered at the man over the barrel of his gun. "So you threatened Su Liao with exposure if she didn't cooperate. I bet she had no idea about her ancestry until you told her."

"That's right," Zhao grinned. "It almost killed her when she found out. The shame. The dishonor. But it was worth it. When she confronted her adopted parents, it scared the hell out of them. They tried to go into hiding, but I was ready. I arranged for them to be arrested as Uyghur sympathizers. After that, Sabir, or Su Liao, if you prefer, became my pawn. With her parents held hostage, she had no choice. Her will was broken. She made sure my Type 093 submarine could not be tracked across the Pacific. I couldn't have done it without her.

"But you didn't factor Chen into the equation," Caine replied. "He knew what you were up to from the start. He got to Su Liao, and used her against you."

"And now he is using you against me. Tell me Caine, how did Chen manipulate you? What kind of leverage does he have?"

Caine's thoughts turned to Rebecca and Jack as he considered Zhao's question. Their lives depended on what he did next. In the end, this wasn't about Su, or Zhao, or submarines... It was time to finish this. He glanced out at the water, checking on the tiny boat that carried Li Li and the children away.

It was a moment of distraction, a fraction of a second. But that was all Zhao required. He swept up with his fishing knife. He moved fast, clearly well trained in weapons and hand-to-hand combat. Caine fired, but the man's strike had knocked his gun off axis... the shot roared past Zhao's head. Blood sprayed from his ear as the bullet tore through skin and cartilage.

Zhao grunted in pain, most likely deafened by the near miss. But he kept moving, slashing the knife across Caine's forearm. A crimson gash erupted across his skin. His fingers spasmed as pain shot through the nerves in his hand and wrist. The gun fell from his weakened grip, clattering across the deck.

Zhao swung again. The blade powered through the air, plunging towards Caine's heart.

Caine sidestepped just in time. The blow missed, but he slammed into the boat's sidewall, losing his balance in the process. Zhao spun around, landing a kick that knocked him over the railing.

Caine felt himself tumbling, falling. As he hit the water, his mask tore loose. He closed his eyes tight, blocking out the shining rush of the ocean.

It took him only a second to get his bearings in the churning water. As he kicked his way to the surface, he realized his pistol was still up on the boat's deck. His speargun was attached to his pack, deeper in the water. He was weaponless.

Wiping the saltwater from his eyes, he heard the boat's motors chug to life. As Zhao motored away from him, he swung the vessel in a wide circle.

BANG! BANG! Tiny explosions erupted from the water around him. Zhao had grabbed his gun... he was shooting at him!

Caine dove. Kicking his way down to the seabed. More bullets pierced the water, leaving long white trails of bubbles in their wake. He had one chance before Zhao made his escape. Caine swam low, skimming across the coral reef. He squinted, ignoring the burning saltwater as he searched for his tactical pack.

But he saw nothing. Only reefs and thousands of fish, eels and sponges. In the sparkling blue water, everything looked the same. He couldn't remember where the detonator was, and without his mask, everything was blurry.

His lungs burned. He was running out of breath. He took one last look, then kicked his way back to the surface.

Gasping for breath, he saw the yacht, completing its wide turn in the distance.

It was coming back.

It was coming for him.

Caine sucked in a deep lungful of air, then dove again. The sea grew dark as the boat streaked above him, blotting out the sunlight. His feet barely cleared the spinning propellers. Looking back, he saw a turbulent mass of bubbles above him. The razor-sharp blades churned the water into a white froth as the boat sped away.

He swam down until he reached the seabed again. But still he saw no sign of his pack.

Maybe it's gone, he thought, *carried away by the current.*

Out of breath, Caine surfaced again.

The yacht was turning again. He knew Zhao would keep coming for him until the propellers tore him to shreds. Even if he managed to evade the deadly blades, he couldn't keep this up forever. Sooner or later, he would drown from exhaustion.

But Zhao didn't know about the explosives strapped to his yacht.

Caine filled his lungs and ducked down again. The yacht rushed over him. This time, Caine's body spun through the water, caught in the turbulence of the propellers. He couldn't see, couldn't tell, which way was up. His breath exploded from his lungs... he had to surface again.

As he bobbed in the water gulping at the air, he heard the boat. Its motors whined as it turned around for another attack.

Gritting his teeth, Caine dove. He knew he was fighting a losing battle, ducking and diving each time Zhao attacked. Zhao could keep coming until he ran out of fuel. But Caine would soon be too exhausted to swim.

He only had one option left. Find his scuba gear and the detonator.

He crawled through the water, trying to spot landmarks that could guide him to his equipment. He swam in circles, moving out from a central point, but even that was difficult to do. The minutes ticked by.

Finally he saw something. A beam of light from above, glinting off metal.

Before he could swim any closer, he felt his lungs heave and burn. He needed more air. He forced himself to surface.

As his head broke through the choppy water, he saw the yacht in the distance. Its motor chugged, but it sat motionless in the water, like a moray eel waiting for its prey to swim too close.

As Caine gasped for more breath, he saw Zhao standing on the deck, searching with binoculars.

Caine ducked back into the water and dove again. He didn't know if Zhao had spotted him, but he didn't intend to wait and find out. He zeroed in on the scuba gear, and swam straight for it. The distance was further than he expected. He was slower now, and his muscles ached with exhaustion. His lungs were already burning, as his body depleted oxygen at an accelerated rate.

The shimmering silver tanks grew closer in his vision. He was almost there... He kicked harder, ignoring the pain in his chest. His fingers brushed against the smooth, curved metal cylinders of the tanks. He grabbed the scuba gear's floating regulator, placed it in his mouth, and took a breath. A curtain of bubbles expelled from the mouthpiece as he exhaled.

He had done it.

He took a few more breaths, then slipped the tank over his body. He heard the yacht's engines, muted and distant through the water. Zhao had given up... he was fleeing. Caine was running out of time.

He rummaged through his tactical pack for the detonator. His flippers were still on the yacht and he had lost his mask, but he'd gladly give up both items for the scuba tank any day. His fingers closed around the tiny blinking detonator. Looking up, he saw the boat pass overhead.

Too close, he thought. *Got to put some distance between us.*

Caine swam, headed east towards the coast of Nusa Penida, staying a few meters below the surface. When he had covered several hundred meters, he surfaced. He hung below the water line, giving himself a few moments at that depth to decompress. Then he kicked back to the surface.

The yacht was far behind him now, and speeding away from the area. In a few seconds, he knew it would be out of range.

Caine wrapped his fingers around the remote radio-controlled detonator. He raised it above the water, and flicked off the safety switch. Then pressed down on the red detonation button.

In the distance, a massive explosion ballooned beneath the surface of the water. The yacht tore into three pieces, as a series of brilliant fireballs erupted across the deck. Then, as if in slow motion, the burning debris flew up into the air. The fragments of the yacht vanished within a rising plume of frothing white water.

For a few moments, the water seemed to hang in the air, like a storm cloud heavy with rain. Then it fell back to the sea, pelting the surface with bits of mangled wood and metal.

The boat was gone, annihilated by the blasts. Caine watched as the remaining fragments sank beneath the waves. Within seconds they were gone, claimed forever by the shimmering blue depths. A bitter smile crossed his lips.

He knew Zhao's fate would be no different.

CHAPTER THIRTY-TWO

CHANGI AIRPORT, SINGAPORE

Thomas Caine, Su Liao and Jezebel Yan stood in silence on the edge of the tarmac, as the Chinese cargo plane taxied across the runway. Behind them, a group of CIA paramilitary officers stood ready and waiting. The next few minutes would prove decisive. They could set into motion a series of events that could have profound consequences for both American and Chinese intelligence operatives across the globe.

Caine swallowed. It was hot and humid in Singapore. Even though it was early morning, his skin glistened with a sheen of sweat. He had done all he could to save Rebecca and Tyler, as well as Su Liao's parents. All he had been able to do since Bali was wait. He watched the plane come to a halt with an intense, smoldering stare. There was no telling what tortures and other horrors they had endured over the last six days. Caine clenched his right hand into a fist.

If Rebecca had been harmed... He forced the dark cloud from his mind, as the passenger door of the plane swung open.

The first to step off the plane were an elderly Asian couple. They struggled to walk, even to hold themselves upright. Their blue pajama-like prison uniforms were threadbare and soiled. The CIA's SOG paramilitary operations officers took chain of custody, and checked them over. After they were cleared, a medical team stepped in, offering first aid complete with wheelchairs, bandages and IV drips.

"Are they your parents?" Yan asked Su, crossing her arms and narrowing her gaze. Like him, she would have to learn to live with the consequences of this operation, whatever they might be.

Su nodded. Silent tears rushed down Su Liao's cheeks. She stood between Caine and Yan, as if shielding herself from the others on the tarmac.

"They are so thin." She turned to Yan, who gave her a nod.

Su was about to step forward when Yan grabbed her by the elbow. "Su, wait," the CIA Station Head warned. "Remember, they may have been indoctrinated. They will have been told many false stories about you. Maybe while under torture."

Su pulled away from her arm. "What is that supposed to mean?"

"It means this may not be the reunion you hope for. It will take time."

Su turned and marched across the tarmac. The mother looked up, and seemed to recognize Su immediately. She threw her arms open and embraced her daughter. They held each other tight, not letting go. Soon the father joined the group hug. Caine could hear their sobs, building in intensity. Then Su turned, and he saw her smiling. Her face seemed to light up. She was weeping tears of joy.

"Maybe things are better than you hoped, Ma'am," Caine said in a low voice.

Yan did not respond. She merely watched the family in silence.

Rebecca and Tyler were next out of the plane. They supported each other as they staggered across the tarmac. Their baggy prison uniforms hung off their bodies. Even from a distance, Caine saw multiple bruises on their arms and faces. There was no doubt... someone had beat them during their incarceration.

The SOG operations officers made a quick inspection of Rebecca and Tyler, checking for any unexpected surprises. It was not unheard of for foreign powers to hide bombs or biological weapons in the bodies of prisoners. But the two were soon cleared, and offered wheelchairs for their trip to the nearest hospital.

Meanwhile the Shaanxi was already taxiing back to the runway. The pilots had no intention of remaining any longer than necessary.

Yan nodded to Rebecca. The medical team was inserting a saline drip into a vein on her arm. "You better go to her."

Caine nodded and stepped forward. As the ambulance carrying Su and her parents pulled away, he jogged over to Rebecca's side. She said nothing as he reached out and grabbed her hand. She just grabbed back and held on tight.

"I'm sorry," were the only words he could think to say.

Rebecca nodded and burst into tears. He held her tight. As she nuzzled her head into his shoulder he watched Tyler in his wheelchair. Paramedics were taking him to another ambulance.

Jack looked like he had taken a beating, and his skin had that grey hue that only came with malnutrition. But he still managed to give Caine the thumbs up.

Caine grinned, and returned the gesture.

"We need to get these two to the hospital," the paramedic said to Caine.

Caine nodded and walked alongside Rebecca. He climbed up into the ambulance as they lifted her chair, and maneuvered her next to Tyler.

He would stay with them for as long as they needed him.

―――

By mid-afternoon the doctors at Singapore General Hospital gave their four patients a clean bill of health. Caine stayed with Rebecca in her private room. She was exhausted, her face gaunt and ashen. Doctors had given her a broad range of antibiotics and various updates for her vaccinations. The quiet drip of the IV was the only sound in the otherwise silent room.

Rebecca drifted in and out of sleep. Caine held her hand. He sat next to her in silence, but inside, his rage simmered and grew. His eyes held a dangerous, predatory glare. Doctors and nurses avoided his gaze when they checked in on her.

Chen Fa Li, he thought. He was responsible. He had done this to her, and to Jack.

He would pay.

It took a moment for Caine to realize Rebecca's eyes were open and she was watching him.

He took her hand to his mouth and kissed her.

"I'm sorry," she spoke weakly.

"What are you sorry about?"

"I lied to you."

Caine nodded. "You told me you were going to Portugal."

She looked away. "Someone had to go. Your cover was blown in China, Tom."

"I don't need you to protect me." He didn't mean them to, but his words sounded harsh. Angry.

Rebecca nodded and held his stare. "I realize that now. In Maui, I saw the beating your body had taken. I read your after-action report, too. You were tortured in Tumaco. But you never talked about it."

Caine was silent. He didn't know how to answer her. His special forces training had conditioned him to keep going, no matter what. Put everything behind him, focus on the here and now. He hadn't realized he had applied that training to every aspect of his life, including his relationship with Rebecca.

Tears rolled down Rebecca's cheeks. "I don't know how you do it. I mean, I've been trained to resist torture and interrogation, but you can only hold out so long. I didn't last a day."

"It's okay," he said squeezing her hand. "It's over now."

"I'll be fine," she said defiantly. Anger was bubbling up inside her too.

"I know you will."

"But I learnt something important in Xinjiang."

Caine raised an eyebrow. He wasn't certain he wanted to hear what Rebecca was about to say.

"Tom, Chen used our relationship against us. He has been since the beginning. He knew I was stationed in Hong Kong. That's how he knew you'd be there too."

"He did," Caine said, nodding in agreement and reflecting on recent events. "The backdoor into the PLA Navy's submarine program has been patched, by the way. Chen knew about it all along."

Rebecca nodded. "We can still use Su Liao. She'll still be able to teach us about China's naval systems. In the end, you were right. She was the real deal."

Caine said nothing. He just stroked her hand. After a few minutes, she spoke again.

"Jezebel Yan has asked me to come back to Hong Kong. She wants me to work with her there. I'll be back to my old job. A senior analyst working on Yan's team."

Caine nodded. "It's what you always wanted."

"Tom, that day, in Hong Kong... When you told me I should stay, even if you had to leave?"

He smiled. "I remember."

She turned her head to face him. Her eyes were groggy and her pupils dilated, but her voice was clear and alert. "I never wanted that, Tom. That was never an option for me. I guess I was just hurt that you thought it was. I told Yan, I would only take the post if she could find a way to get you cleared again. Yan's smart. Maybe she can figure something out, make a deal. And if she can't, then..." Her voice trailed off to a whisper. Her eyes fluttered closed.

Then they snapped open again. "We can't keep hiding our pain," she murmured. "We think we're protecting each other. But we're not.

We're just... running in circles. If we're going to be together, you have... to stop hiding, Tom. You have to let me in."

Caine nodded, and patted her hand. "We'll talk about it later. Just get some rest."

He didn't tell her that Yan had already spoken to him. That he had told her no. That they had both agreed the best thing for Rebecca was to get as far away from him as possible.

He looked away, as Rebecca rested her head on her pillow and fell back asleep.

The rage inside him had been growing in intensity since Bali.

Now it was time to release it.

CHAPTER THIRTY-THREE

WEST VIRGINIA, UNITED STATES

Su Liao ran.

She ran for kilometers. She ran for hours. She ran until her legs ached, until the physical pain was greater than her emotional anguish.

Her nights were restless. By day she could distract herself with work, or her exercise regime. But when she lay down for bed, engulfed by the cold, dark emptiness of nightfall… that was when the nightmares came. She would wake up screaming, tears streaking down her face. She would tremble and shiver for hours, until her exhausted body finally slipped back into unconsciousness.

The lack of sleep was taking a toll. She barely ate. Her stomach seemed to be in a constant state of distress. The few times she dared to look at herself in the mirror, all she saw was a ghost staring back at her. A pale, wasted shadow of the woman she thought she should have been.

But still, she forced herself to run. Rebecca had suggested she make a morning run part of her ritual, to help relieve stress. Now, it was the only thing that brought her peace. As she powered through the mountain trails, sunlight streamed through the red pine and spruce forest. Her feet pounded over a soft carpet of fallen needles covering the earth. Misty vapor puffed from her mouth and nostrils as she panted for breath. She forced her arms and legs to keep moving, and considered her predicament.

Everything had worked out as she hoped. Better, in fact. Physically, her parents had recovered, and they seemed like their old selves again. The three of them lived in a nice home in town, paid for by the United States government. They all had new identities. Her parents spent their days tinkering in the garden. And Su ran.

She had been running for three months.

She was paid a salary by the CIA. The backdoor into the PLA Navy's submarine navigation program was closed now. The CIA could no longer use her to track the movements of Chinese submarines. But they still consulted with her on the coding, strategies, protocols and conventions of the PLA's information network system. She helped analysts at the NSA and the CIA hack into Chinese systems wherever they could. Su was still useful, valuable. And they trusted her and her family enough to not only let them live without minders, but in a home of their own.

Life, had never been better.

But Su knew it wouldn't last.

When Chen Fa Li appeared on the path before her, she almost wasn't surprised. He was standing alone, in the middle of the trail. The sunlight illuminated against the haze of frost-filled air. He looked like a shadow at first, a silhouette against the white snow and frost-covered pines. He wore a trench coat and a two-piece suit. He was dressed like an American. The one aspect of his physical appearance that never changed was his sleek, stylish hair, always parted on his left side. He stepped forward and gave a practiced smile. He looked like a politician, or a news anchor. But Su knew he was far more dangerous than that.

She stopped running. Her breath caught in her throat. It made a tiny, strangled sound, a cross between a gasp and a sigh.

"I see you running here almost every day," Chen Fa Li said in a pleasant voice. "I wonder how you find time to do anything else?"

Su's heart was pounding. Her breath out of control. Her legs were starting to feel like jelly. There was no chance she could answer him.

Chen came forward and brushed his hand across Su's soft cheek. He stared at her, but there was no affection in his eyes. He looked at her like a man might look upon a beautiful painting, or a classic sports car. To him, she was an asset. A possession. As far as he was concerned, he owned her.

The worst part was, Su knew he was right. She could not bring herself to look into his eyes.

"Are you ready to work for me again?" he asked quietly.

Su trembled.

"Remember all our long talks, little one? Remember how I taught you how to manipulate Caine, convince Yan and Freeling that you could be of use to them? Remember how you promised that if I got your parents out of Xinjiang, if I saved you from Zhao, you'd work for me?"

She nodded.

He grabbed her hair violently and yanked her head up, forcing her to meet his stare. "Now is the time to honor your promises, Liao. Zhao Jianyu was a problem for all of us. If he sold the Colombian cocaine as planned, his power in China would have increased a hundredfold. We couldn't have that, could we?"

She shook her head enthusiastically. Or perhaps Chen did it for her. She no longer knew anymore. Her life was not her own. It had not been for some time.

"Say it!" Chen spat out the words.

Su swallowed. "I..."

"SAY IT!" He shouted. She cried out as he pulled harder on her hair.

"I belong to you," she almost choked on her words. "You... own me."

"Excellent." He released her, then brushed away the strands of hair that had fallen across her eyes. "We understand each other, then. Dead drops will be arranged. That is how you will receive mission objectives. You will work towards a permanent position with the NSA, or failing that, the CIA. This is a long game, Liao. If you fail me, Jezebel Yan will be sent video files of our little talks. She will see you pledging your loyalty to me, promising to work as a double agent for the glory of China. She too, will see that I own—"

An explosive crack, like the sound of a whip, echoed through the forest. Su screamed and pulled away from Chen's grip.

She took a step backwards, as Chen's eyes rolled up into the back of his head. A crimson hole had opened in the side of his skull. Blood gushed from the wound. The man crumpled, fell like a puppet with his strings cut.

Su froze in place. She was too terrified to move, too scared to even blink. She felt pinpricks of heat on her face... she realized Chen's blood was spattered across her skin.

Another man stepped onto the path. His charcoal coat and dark jeans were dusted with snow. His hiking boots gouged deep prints in the frosted earth as he walked towards her. He was tall, with thick brown hair and eyes the color of jade gemstones. In his hand he held a smoking semi-automatic pistol.

Thomas Caine stepped up to Chen's body and fired two more shots into his chest. Su shuddered with each gunshot. The silence after was even more terrifying. She feared the next shot might be for her.

As the echo of the last shot faded to a distant murmur, Caine looked up at her. When she looked into his blazing green eyes, she was certain... He had heard her conversation with Chen. He knew.

She dropped to her knees, closed her eyes. She had been living in fear for so long, even after she was safely in America, with her parents by her side. Anything would be better than this. Even death.

"Please let my parents live?" she begged, squeezing her eyes shut. "They have done nothing wrong."

She wondered if she would feel the hot metal barrel on the back of her head before the end came.

Instead she felt a warm, calloused hand take hers, and help her onto her feet.

"Open your eyes," Caine said coldly. "I'm not here to kill you. Or your parents."

Su sobbed, and staggered to her feet.

She watched as Caine patted down Chen's corpse. "He... he would not have come alone," she said in a hesitant, halting voice. "There may be others—"

"He came with three other men," Caine snapped. "They're all dead now."

She remained silent as he finished searching the body. He found nothing of interest.

"You're not going to kill me?" she finally asked.

He stood and looked her up and down. "No," he said with a finality that scared her, despite it being the answer she hoped for. "I would have done exactly the same, in your circumstances. But there are consequences."

"What do you mean?"

He looked at her, his piercing green eyes both terrifying and compassionate at the same time. "You can't stay in America. If anyone other than me finds out you were working for Chen, playing both sides, you'll end up in Federal prison. Maybe worse."

Su shivered. Now that she wasn't running, the cold was seeping through her clothes, chilling her to the bone.

Caine reached into his pocket. He withdrew an envelope and placed it into her hands. He closed her trembling fingers around the package, ensuring she had a firm grip. "Inside are three Canadian passports, with matching credit cards. And enough cash to get you into Canada and set up a new life. The contact who prepared these is very discreet, and not part of my government."

"Why are you doing this?" she eventually asked.

Caine was silent for a moment as he considered his answer. "You've had an awful life... Aynur Sabir."

She shuddered at Caine's words. That was a name she had not heard in a very long time. Her first name. Her real name.

"Zhao told me," he continued. "You are Uyghur. Your adoptive parents were very brave, protecting you for as long as they could. And you protected them in return."

"But... but I was going to betray you," she stammered.

Caine shook his head. "Nature of the game. You got yourself and your family out of an impossible situation. Like I said, I would have done the same myself. But Chen, the people you were working with... they caused my friends a lot of pain. If I ever see you ever again... I won't protect you. Do you understand?"

She nodded. "So what do we do? Just get in the car, and drive north into Canada? Start all over again?"

Caine nodded. "That's exactly what you do. Rent a new car. Use the cards in that envelope, not your old ones. Leave everything else behind, including your cell phones. They can be tracked."

She clutched her body, hugging herself for warmth. "Thank you, Mr. Caine. I know I don't deserve this. But I thank you anyway." She gave a tiny bow.

He turned to leave, but stopped, and turned around. "You'll be alright, Su. You know what you're doing. You've been hiding your whole life. I hope wherever you end up, you can stop running. Live your life, enjoy the time you have left. Spend it with the people you love."

Then he turned and walked away. His footsteps crunched against the snow, as he vanished into the frost-filled air.

———

After he disposed of the bodies, Caine drove deep into the Virginian forests. He needed time to think. Time to be alone.

He parked his SUV, and walked aimlessly among the shadows of the towering trees. He lost track of how far he meandered, but eventually he found himself standing beside a rushing river. The cool water cascaded over rocks, surrounded by magnificent pine trees and the mountain peaks in the distance. The scene was serene and peaceful, but Caine didn't feel either of those emotions.

Rebecca was back in Hong Kong now. She had taken the posting, after she recovered from her torture at Chen's hands. Her career as a senior analyst in the Far East division was on the fast track. Despite her young age, she was doing better than most intelligence officers with three times as much experience as her.

Their parting had been difficult. Harsh words, bitter tears... She had not given in easily. But like all wounds, the pain had lessoned with time. She was there, and he was here. That was all there was to it.

It was what he had wanted, what he knew needed to happen. But it didn't change the emptiness he felt. The cold, dead space in his heart that she had once helped fill had returned. He felt numb, and hollow inside. But he knew things could be worse... Worse for both of them.

He thought back to his time with her in the hospital. The bruises and cuts on her skin. Rebecca's words, spoken in a drugged, half-conscious daze... *"Chen used our relationship against us."*

He had told Su that Chen had caused his friends great pain. But even as the words left his mouth, he knew that was a lie. Chen had used Rebecca and Jack to get to him.

It's your fault, he thought. *Your fault they suffered.*

That day in the hospital, he vowed it would never happen again.

Like Su, he had been hiding, shielding himself from the truth. But not anymore. No matter how much he wanted her, no matter how empty he felt inside... He knew it was time to let go.

He felt the key in his pocket, the gift he had planned on giving her in Hawaii. He had planned to ask her to move in with him. But that was impossible now.

Maybe, he thought. Maybe someday when this life of shadows and sacrifice was a faded memory. Maybe then they might work things out, try again.

Or maybe not.

His cell phone rang. He recognized the number. It was Jack Tyler.

"Hey kid. Been trying to reach you for hours."

Caine had dismantled his cell phone while he dealt with Su Liao and Chen Fa Li. He didn't want anyone tracking his movements. "Jack," he said, "Sorry. Wanted to lay low for a while."

"Vacation's over, partner. How far away are you from Ronald Reagan Airport? You and I have a flight to catch, ASAP."

"Another mission?"

"You bet your ass."

Caine couldn't help but grin, despite his melancholy. "Don't worry. I'll be there."

He disconnected the call and pocketed his phone.

He took one last look at the dark, rushing water. He inhaled the cool mountain air. It smelled of damp earth and pine. The scent calmed him.

He reached into his pocket and pulled out the keys. Keys Rebecca would never know could have been hers. A life she was better off without. He weighed them in his hand for a moment, then threw them as far as he could into the rushing water.

Caine turned and marched back down the hill. As he descended into the trees, a cloud shifted across the sun, and the light dimmed. Behind him, long dark shadows stretched across the cold, powdered earth.

The river continued to burble its soothing tune. The dark water carried the shiny bits of metal onward, down the mountain. They tumbled towards whatever grave awaited the death of future dreams.

THOMAS CAINE RETURNS IN...

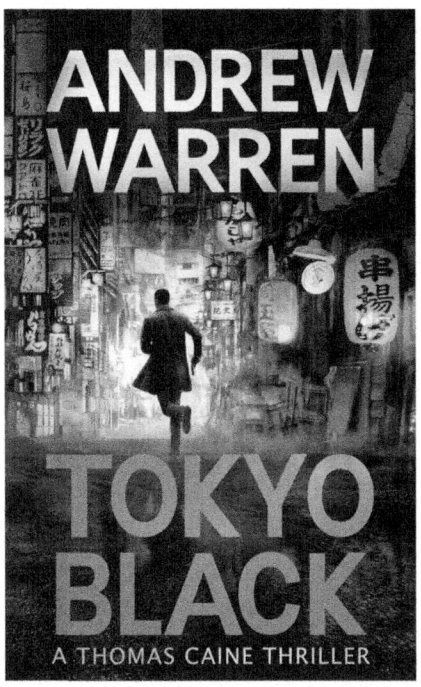

A betrayed assassin. A terrorist cult. A secret that could plunge America and Japan into chaos...

Turn the page for a FREE sample...

TOKYO BLACK - CHAPTER ONE

The pulsing neon lights of Shinjuku made the darkness of the alley seem even more black and desolate, like the cold, empty space between stars. A lone figure crept down the narrow passage. He stopped just before the edge of the shadows, peering out cautiously at the lights and commotion ahead. Like many streets in the East Mouth shopping district, this one was for pedestrians only. The throng of people passing before him was like a river of bodies. They pushed, jostled, and raged forward, a relentless force of nature in pursuit of the city's pleasures.

Tatsui Kentaro was dressed in a rumpled grey suit, the typical uniform of a Tokyo sarariman. Legions of these low-status, middle-income office workers filled the office buildings of Japan like drones in a beehive. Thick, black glasses pinched the bridge of his nose. Their lenses magnified his sunken brown eyes.

Tatsui brought a lit cigarette to his lips. He took a long, slow drag, then held it in front of him for a second, staring at the twin gold bands of the Mevius label. He shook his head, dropped the cigarette, and ground it beneath his heel. Running a hand through his salt-and-pepper hair, he looked left and right, checking the alley exit. No one in the massive crowd outside was paying any attention to him.

He laughed to himself. After twenty-five years of marriage, his wife was hardly concerned with his comings and goings anymore. The kids were grown adults now. Tatsui and his wife had reached the stage where infidelity was a tacit compromise, rather than a painful betrayal. Still, old habits die hard, and he couldn't help but be wary as he pushed his way into the throng before him.

Tatsui sniffed at the crisp night air. Grilled meats, garlic, fried noodles ... the enticing scents of yakitori reached out to him, comforting and seductive at the same time. For a moment, he considered stopping; it had been hours since he'd finished the small bento box lunch his wife had packed for him.

Instead, he stuck his hands in the pockets of his beige raincoat, hunched his shoulders, and pulled the coat tighter against the cold. He had other appetites to fulfill. And after hours of overtime in a cramped office, the illicit promises of Kabukicho's many temptations filled his gut with tingling excitement.

His anticipation grew as he passed the massive TV screen of Studio Alta. The giant display towered above the street, blasting the night sky with colorful images of anime and Japanese soap opera stars. The landmark provided a popular meeting spot for the area. As he ambled on, Tatsui watched couples embrace, teenagers laugh and roughhouse, and girls trade cell phone charms and gossip.

But for Tatsui, Studio Alta was something else ... a signpost. He was close now.

The pedestrian street crossed over Yasukuni-dori and led the sarariman to a large archway of flashing red lights. This was the gateway to Kabukicho, the most infamous neighborhood in Shinjuku and, indeed, all of Japan.

Here, the neon lights and signs continued to defy the darkness, but the services they advertised were of a different nature. The streets were lined with hostess clubs, massage parlors, pachinko halls... Tatsui lit another cigarette and resumed his journey into the night.

An attractive Japanese woman dressed as a maid stood at the corner near Bunka-Senta dori, passing out flyers. "Massagee, massagee?" she asked, her voice high-pitched and giggly.

Tatsui bowed and took a flyer, but he did not stop walking. His appetite led him elsewhere.

He continued past a group of what he assumed to be yakuza thugs camped outside a pachinko parlor. Clad in expensive suits, their wide-collared shirts exposed the ink of tattoos around their necks. They watched him with cold eyes and humorless smiles. Tatsui knew they would not harass him unless he owed them money, but they made him nervous nonetheless.

He hurried on, past the karaoke bars and the host club with the young, bleached blond men on the sign. Past the love hotels with their flashing pink hearts and teddy bears signs. Past the strip clubs, where the girls were Filipino, Chinese, even Russian, but almost never Japanese. Then past the old, rundown batting cages, where you could work out your tension swinging at balls or playing the old pornographic mahjong video game in the back room.

Finally, almost suddenly, Tatsui stopped. The crowd seemed to part around him as he smiled at a pink neon sign on the balcony of the building before him.

"*Shiro Kumo Tengoku*," it read. White Cloud Heaven. Images of beautiful Japanese women surrounded the kanji characters. Their naked bodies were strategically covered in sparkling white soapsuds. Tatsui gazed into their unseeing eyes and took a deep drag of his cigarette. He looked around again, making sure no one was paying any attention to his activities. He knew no one was, but he enjoyed the little intrigue, the imagined risk. It made the excitement of what was to come even sweeter.

Satisfied that he was just another anonymous pleasure-seeker in the night, Tatsui dropped his cigarette to the ground. Then he pushed through the front door and stepped into heaven.

DEPTH CHARGE

Twenty minutes later, Tatsui lay on his back while a beautiful girl moved her hands across his body with slow, firm motions. She was naked, as was he. She said her name was Yuki, and she was a twenty-year-old college student. He knew none of this was true, of course. But he didn't care. Her body was warm and taut, her hair was thick and dark, and her face reminded him of an angel.

After he'd chosen her from a wall of pictures in the lobby below, she'd led him hand in hand to this warm but clinical room, where they had both stripped naked. After a warm bath in the Roman tub and a vigorous body scrub, they had moved to an air mattress on the floor. Then the evening's real entertainment had begun.

Tatsui smiled as Yuki ceased her massage, satisfied that he was aroused and ready for the next step. She dipped her hands into a bowl full of clear liquid gel. With soft, circular motions, she began to spread the warm, slippery substance across his body.

She gave Tatsui a sexy grin as she lowered herself onto him and began to slide her body up and down and across his own. The gel, known as Nuru, acted like a lubricant. It turned every movement of her body into a long, slow massage stroke.

Her small, perfect body glided down the length of his limbs as her pert breasts pressed into his flesh. Tatsui made a sound that was part moan, part joyous laughter. He was in heaven. The pleasure of the Nuru massage was like nectar, feeding him, making him feel alive. His body—old, tired, worn down, and battered—felt sleek and new.

Yuki giggled. He felt her intense heat as she clamped her legs around his and continued her gliding dance of pleasure. He was close now, and the girl was an expert. She intensified her movements, concentrating her warmth and friction on the focal point of his pleasure.

A loud crash echoed from the hall outside the room. Tatsui, lost in a sea of bliss, barely heard the noise. Yuki gasped and froze in place.

Jolted from his dreamlike trance, Tatsui propped himself up on the air mattress. He could hear muted shouting and footsteps coming from the other side of the door. He looked up at Yuki with alarm.

"What the hell is going on? Cops?"

Yuki shook her head. "Can't be. We pay the yakuza for protection. Hurry, get dressed!" She slid off him and threw on a pink silk robe.

Tatsui scrambled off the mattress and grabbed his clothes. Ignoring his underwear, he struggled to pull on his suit pants. His legs were sticky from the massage gel, and the fabric tangled around his ankles.

Tatsui looked up when he heard the sound of doors breaking, followed by a high-pitched scream. The noises were close now, and the commotion outside grew louder. He heard girls shrieking, men shouting, and customers complaining.

Yuki hid behind him as he finally buttoned his pants. The door flew open, showering wood splinters through the air. Yuki wailed as men in black suits poured into the room, their faces cold but determined.

One of the men grabbed the struggling Yuki and dragged her from the room. Tatsui realized with a start that they were all carrying guns.

Tatsui had never seen a firearm before, at least not in person. The police didn't carry them, and even yakuza gangsters rarely displayed them in public. Before, he had worried that police or federal agents were cracking down on the soaplands brothel. He had feared that he might be arrested and have to explain his activities to his wife. Now a cold, sickening fear filled his gut as he realized things were worse.

Much worse.

The two thugs who manhandled him from the room were dressed from head to toe in black. Black suits, black shirts, black shoes, black socks. One had left the top buttons of his shirt open, exposing hideous burn-like scars across his chest.

"Please, there's no need for this! I'll give you whatever you want, whatever I have," Tatsui babbled.

They ignored him as they dragged him to the lounge at the end of the hall. There, a group of naked clients and petrified girls huddled together. Yuki and two other girls lay on the floor, staring up at another black-suited man. His back was to Tatsui, but the terrified sarariman could tell he was huge. His broad shoulders looked like a wall of black granite.

"That's everyone," said one of the suits.

The monster nodded but did not turn around. He was showing a cell phone to the girls.

Yuki shook her head. "No, please, sir. We have not seen her. I swear! Please just leave us alone!"

"Do not lie to me, little one." His voice was like the echo of thunder in a canyon—powerful and booming, but strangely muted.

Yuki closed her eyes and turned away. Tatsui saw the tears streaming down her cheek, now smeared with makeup. Her interrogator raised his giant slab of a hand.

Before the big man struck Yuki, Tatsui spoke. His voice was a dry croak, and the sound of it surprised even himself.

"Please, sir. There is no need for violence. What is it you want?"

The big man lowered his hand and turned around to eye Tatsui. The other thugs immediately trained their guns on him, as if the sound of his voice had caused them to take notice of him for the first time. One clubbed him on the back of his neck with the butt of a rifle, and he collapsed on the floor.

The big man gave Tatsui's attacker a disdainful frown, but he did not offer the injured sarariman any assistance. He looked down impassively. It was the stare of a cold-blooded reptile ... motionless, unfeeling, waiting for prey to move that fraction of an inch too close.

Tatsui picked himself up and stood before the hulking, dark figure. The man's face was a nightmare of strange burns. Twisted scar tissue drew deep, jagged lines through his primitive features. In place of a left eye was a milky, unseeing orb.

Tatsui took a deep breath. "Please, just tell us what you want. If I can help you, I will. Then you can let us go."

The working girls ceased their panicked sobbing. The room grew silent, save for the dim noise of traffic outside.

The big man spoke. "What is your name?"

"Tatsui."

The awful, scarred face gave a small nod, an almost imperceptible tilting of the chin. Still, the motion was at least somewhat human. That comforted Tatsui somewhat. Perhaps there was a chance after all.

"I am called Bobu. I apologize for our rude behavior, but we are on a mission of grave importance. Please, do not be afraid."

Tatsui was dumbfounded by the sharp contrast between the man's smooth, calm words and his horrific face.

Bobu tilted his head, as if focusing the gaze of his injured eye on the man who cowered before him. "Forgive me. I know my scars can be frightening. But know this … they are marks of purity. The heat and fire that made me this way also burned away the shame of my past. Do you understand?"

Tatsui nodded.

Bobu smiled. Tatsui watched the mangled, pink flesh twist and move; smiling was the most terrifying thing the man had done yet.

"We are looking for someone. It is important that we find her as soon as possible. She is lost." Bobu held out the phone to Tatsui.

It showed a picture of a girl in her early twenties. She was sexy and beautiful, like Yuki. But, unlike his masseuse, her beauty was not angelic and carefree. She looked cold, like a porcelain doll. Her dark eyes seemed worried. Haunted.

Color rushed back into the sarariman's features. His eyes lit up with hope. "Yes, yes! I have seen this girl!"

Bobu leaned in, his mutilated face inches away from Tatsui.

"Where?"

"Ah, wait, let me think."

Bobu's cold gaze never wavered as the flustered man racked his brain for details.

Tatsui looked up, a smile on his face. "Yes, I remember! It was in Roppongi, at Tiger Velvet! A hostess club. We were there after work, to celebrate closing a deal. Perhaps ... two weeks ago!"

"You are positive it was her?"

The older man nodded. "Yes, I remember her eyes. She looked unhappy to be there. I told her she should cheer up, and she spilled my sake in my lap! We complained to the manager, and he sent over a different girl."

Bobu stared at him for a few more seconds.

"It was her, I swear!" Tatsui added weakly.

Bobu spun around, and took a few steps away from the crowd. The other men kept their guns trained on Tatsui as the hulking man brought the cell phone to his ear. He spoke in hushed, short sentences. Then he slid the phone in his pocket and turned back to his men.

"Burn it down. No one lives."

Like a switch had been flipped, the room immediately filled with screams and shouts. Tatsui watched in horror as the men opened fire with automatic weapons. Yuki's lifeless face hit the ground. Blood mixed with the black tears of mascara that spattered her face.

He tore away from the men holding him and rushed over to Bobu. "Please, don't do this! We had a deal! Please sir, I have a wife. I have—"

Bobu pushed him away. It was just a light movement of his thick arm, no more than a shrug, but it sent Tatsui sprawling to the floor. In the midst of the massacre, Tatsui smelled gasoline fumes filling the room. A pair of the black-suited killers were dousing the curtains and furniture with cans of the flammable liquid.

Bobu slipped a large pistol from a shoulder holster under his jacket. He leveled the gun at Tatsui's face.

"Don't worry. You will not burn. You will not be purified. You are free."

He pulled the trigger. The gun roared, but Tatsui did not hear it. Or if he did, it was just an echo, a faint fragment of sound trapped in the mists at the edge of his consciousness.

For Tatsui, there was only the growing darkness. For a brief second, he could see the lights of Shinjuku ... brilliant flickering stars, a map of heavenly pleasures on earth. Then, one by one, the stars went out.

TOKYO BLACK - CHAPTER TWO

Mark Waters took a sip of his cocktail and looked over his shoulder at Soi 8, the street outside Lucky's Bar. Late afternoon was always his favorite time in Pattaya. The city seemed to take a deep breath, a relaxing pause before the relentless nightlife whipped the place into a frenzy.

Turning his attention back to the bar, he caught a glimpse of himself in one of the many mirrors hanging on the wall. Years of the intense Pattaya sun had turned his skin a deep tan and lightened his messy brown hair. He knew his prime was past—wrinkles creased his green eyes as he squinted at the image before him. But his navy linen blazer and khaki jeans still fit like a glove. His body was blessed with the lean physique of a natural athlete.

"Your turn, Mr. Waters!"

Janjai, the new bar girl, was grinning at him. Her lively brown eyes held a mischievous gleam, and her beautiful smile was genuine. She had not yet acquired that awful, generic pleasantness like the other bar girls.

Mark didn't blame them. After all, it was their job to entice male tourists into the bar any way they could. Still, after a few months on the scene, the girls learned all the tricks and lines. Their forced smiles, corny greetings, and flirtatious banter grated on his ears every night.

It only bothers you because you can see right through them, he thought. *It's not their fault you're an expert on living a lie.*

"You gonna go or not?" Janjai was staring at him, a friendly pout on her lips. Her crossed arms pressed the coffee-colored skin of her breasts up against the opening of her white tank top. Mark realized she was learning faster than he'd thought.

"Sorry, Jan. Let's see here.... I think you may have got me." Mark examined the Connect Four game that stood between them. The game was a three-dimensional version of Tic-Tac-Toe. The goal was to stack four plastic checkers in a vertical, horizontal, or diagonal row. Janjai's last move had cut off the diagonal line he was building.

He often spent his afternoons playing bar games at Lucky's. He figured it was better for Janjai to earn her money beating him at Connect Four than the other activities she might soon engage in. Most of the time, he let her win.

Today, however, Janjai's inevitable victory was due to her skill alone. With a sigh, he slipped a red checker into the grid. It fell into place, blocking the girl's vertical play, but it left her with an opening to make a horizontal row on her next move.

The Thai girl shrieked with delight as she dropped a black checker into the plastic grid. The piece completed her row of four and won the game. She clapped and laughed. "You lose, Mr. Waters! I too smart for you!"

Mark chuckled as he slipped two hundred baht notes from his wallet and lay them on the counter. Janjai snapped them up with a child-like glee.

"Truer words were never spoken, Janjai. Now, how about you take pity on me and make me a drink?"

"Sure thing, Mr. Waters. Then we play again! You want another sabai sabai?"

"Sounds good to me."

Janjai prepared his drink, a refreshing combination of sugar, lemon, club soda, crushed basil, and local Thai whisky. As she worked, Mark stole a glance at his cell phone. It was a prepaid model from the electronics stand down the street. It showed no incoming calls. *This doesn't feel right*, he thought.

The trucks should have arrived at the docks forty minutes ago. Lau was supposed to check in as soon as they arrived and then again when the merchandise was loaded onboard the boat.

Mark always stayed far away from the docks when a delivery was scheduled to arrive. It was up to his partner, Lau Somchai, to keep him in the loop and confirm that everything was all right. That left two options. Either Lau was keeping him in the dark ... or everything was not all right.

Janjai set the drink down in front of him.

"Ready for next game, Mr. Waters?"

Mark gave her a warm smile and placed another two-hundred baht on the counter. "Give me a few minutes to recover from that last beating, okay? But consider this my reservation."

Janjai nodded and moved away, sensing his wish to be alone. As she wiped down the counter with a wet rag, Mark scanned the bar again. He kept an eye out for Lau or anyone who didn't belong.

His gaze settled on a young Thai man sitting near the railing that separated the open air bar from the street. He was wearing a white dress shirt open at the collar. His sleeves were rolled up, and sweat stained the fabric at the armpits.

He appeared intensely focused on a wrinkled newspaper he was flipping through, an issue of the *Pattaya Times*. He paid no attention to the steady throng of attractive women walking up and down the street outside, many dressed only in bikinis and sarongs.

Mark hadn't noticed him until now. The man had been in the bar for some time, but until this moment, Mark hadn't given him a second thought. He felt wrong somehow. Mark took a deep breath, shocked to realize just how much his skills had atrophied over the past few years.

Keeping a lock on the man from the corner of his eye, Mark angled back towards the bar and took another sip of his cocktail. He let the cold ice linger against his teeth, using the pain to sharpen him up. He allowed himself another unobtrusive glance in the man's direction.

He could just make out the large color photo on the front page of the rumpled newspaper—girls dancing in pink evening gowns. Something about it was familiar.

"Janjai?" he said without looking away, his voice low. "Does Lucifer's Bar still do the beauty pageant thing? You know, where the girls put on fancy dresses and do that fake pageant?"

Janjai leaned over the counter. "Sure. They raffle off the winner for the night. They do that on Wednesday, I think."

It was Saturday afternoon. That meant the man was fully absorbed by two-day-old news.

Mark drained his drink and slammed the glass down on the bar. "Time to make a deposit!" he announced. Janjai giggled but gave him a concerned look. He slipped several baht notes onto the counter. "In case I don't make it back for the game," he whispered. "You probably would have won anyway."

He purposely avoided looking at the Thai man as he made his way to the dingy men's room at the rear of the bar. He staggered and swayed as he walked, giving the impression that he was drunk. With a sigh, he shut himself in the tiny, dark room.

As soon as the door closed, he sprang into action. Tearing his cell phone from his pocket, he popped off the rear cover and disconnected the battery. He threw the battery in the trash and stomped the dead phone into pieces with the heel of his boot. Then he dumped the pieces into a dirty bucket of mop water that stood in a corner. He had no idea who could be tracking him. Based on the lone watcher he'd spotted, it was probably just the Thai Royal Police. But that was far from the only possibility, and the other options could be much more deadly.

Outside the door, he heard Janjai talking. "Please wait, sir. Someone in there!"

Mark uttered a silent curse as footsteps hurried towards the bathroom door. He grabbed a dirty towel that hung from a rack of cleaning supplies and wound it around his arm. Gritting his teeth, he smashed his padded elbow into the dirty glass of the bathroom window. The dusty pane shattered and exploded outwards.

The noise outside grew louder. Janjai was screaming, and someone—most likely the Thai man—was shouting.

Might be calling for backup, Mark thought, *which means if I don't get out now, I don't get out.* Loud thuds echoed through the bathroom as the door shook. Someone was trying to break through.

Mark took a deep breath and vaulted through the broken window into the alley behind the bar. Crouching, he looked up and down the thin strip of dirt. There was a commotion at the south end, the ocean side of town. Five armed men in civilian dress rushed around the corner, charging towards him. One dropped to his knees to take aim with a pistol. Mark launched into an all-out sprint as the weapon roared behind him. The bullets struck the dirt, sending a small cloud of dust into the air near his ankles.

Ducking around the corner of Lucky's Bar, he hurtled into the crowded street of Soi 8. He ran north, away from the beach. A motorized growl grew closer and closer as he ran. A three-wheeled tuk tuk followed close behind, weaving through the pedestrians and bicycles. The tiny vehicle bore the yellow and purple markings of the Thai Royal Police. Three uniformed officers rode onboard.

This is all wrong.

Mark increased his pace, sprinting towards a narrow alley that led towards Soi 7. *Since when do the Royal Police give a damn about some counterfeit jeans and designer purses?* He looked back. Unable to fit down the narrow passage, the tuk tuk had turned away. Mark figured it was probably headed down the boulevard that linked Soi 8 and Soi 7.

Panting, Mark burst out the other end of the alley and turned north again, heading up Soi 7. Behind him, he heard the tiny vehicle screech around the corner; the driver must have anticipated his route. A wailing siren now rose above the whine of the tiny motor.

Pedestrians and motor scooters swerved left and right, clearing the street for the police as they closed the gap. Mark gasped for breath, knowing it was only a matter of time before they caught up to him. Even at his peak, now several years behind him, he couldn't run like this forever.

A small truck pulled into the cross street ahead of him. The driver leaned on his horn, trying to clear the throng of pedestrians from the crosswalk ahead.

Mark dropped to the ground and slid under the truck. The rough pavement tore at his clothes and scraped his skin. Ignoring the pain, he rolled out from under the other side of the vehicle and leapt to his feet. He turned and continued his frenzied run.

Behind him, the tuk tuk driver slammed on the brakes, but he was too close and traveling too fast. The tiny vehicle fishtailed in the street, sending the crowd of partygoers clambering to the sidewalks. The passengers leapt from the unstable vehicle as it rolled onto its side and slammed into the truck.

Mark couldn't resist the slightest grin of satisfaction. He dodged to the left and ran into an outdoor beer garden. Finally, he had gained some distance on his pursuers. The sirens and shouting grew fainter as he lost himself in the crowd.

Mark stood in a shadowy corner of the Venus Club, a sleek, modern structure of glass and chrome, built to resemble a popular bar in Bangkok. The bar's interior was a sci-fi fantasy: each of the club's go-

go dancers held a laser pointer, which they flashed around the room as they slithered and swayed atop their chrome pedestals.

The glass-enclosed bar was suspended above a parking garage in the wealthy, modern neighborhood of Amaya Hill. Several beautiful Thai girls danced near the edge of the structure, grinding their bodies against the clear walls. They aimed their lasers at the pedestrians below, hoping to lure more young, rich partygoers into the club.

Ignoring the beams of light dancing over his body, Mark scanned the crowd from a second-level catwalk. The height gave him a bird's eye view of the girls and their customers, and the shadows helped hide his torn, dirty clothes. He had been able to avoid the police so far, but he knew they were still looking for him. He would have to keep a low profile until he could get out of the city.

Still early in the evening, the crowd was sparse. As he surveyed the room, he spotted the man he had been looking for. Lau Somchai.

He watched as the short, chubby man ambled into the club, laughing and gesturing expansively with his arms. He wore a loud Hawaiian shirt and expensive-looking slacks. The bar girls immediately marked him as "money" and began moving closer, teasing their laser beams across his body. The lights danced across his partner's face. Mark saw quick flashes of greasy, pockmarked skin and dark, beady eyes.

Lau peeled off baht notes from a shiny money clip and tossed them onto the bar with a flourish. The bartenders set up a round of drinks for Lau and the lingerie-clad girls that surrounded him. All the girls were beautiful, but Mark knew Lau's favorite was Kandi. Within minutes, the waif-like Thai-Filipino girl was at his side. She laughed and ran her hands across Lau's sweaty, bald head while whispering into his ear.

Lau threw down some more money, then took Kandi's hand as she led him up the metal stairs to the catwalk. Mark left his perch for one of the small glass rooms that surrounded the slender stage. *It's only a matter of time now*, he thought. Hopefully he'd paid Kandi more than Lau had.

Inside the room were dark velvet curtains, and Mark drew them closed. Outside, the loud beats of dance music overrode all other sound. The bass washed over his body like an ocean wave, penetrating him to the core, shaking his bowels and organs. Mark stood motionless in the corner next to the door, waiting in the darkness.

He didn't flinch when the door opened, even though he could neither hear nor see anyone approach. Two shadowy figures appeared: Kandi and Lau. *Should have paid more for the lap dance, you cheap bastard!*

Mark let Lau walk past him before emerging from his corner. He slid his body between the short, pudgy man and Kandi. Before either Lau or the dancer could react, Mark lifted his right foot and stomped down hard on the inside of Lau's knee. With a surprised grunt, Lau lurched forward and tripped. He landed face-first on the plush velvet couch that dominated the room.

"Take a seat, partner."

Mark kept his back neutral, not wanting to give Kandi an opportunity to betray him. He turned and saw that the petite brunette in purple lingerie hadn't even entered the room. Mark held up a wad of bills. "Thank you," he said. There was no warmth in his voice.

Kandi blinked as a barrage of green lasers flashed over their faces through the open door. She took one look at Mark's cold, hard eyes, grabbed the money, and hurried off. He swung back to face Lau.

He shut the door to the room, muting the music outside. Lau gasped and groaned as he pulled himself up to a seated position on the couch. Mark pulled aside a curtain, letting a crack of light into the room. When Lau saw his face, the look of confused anger melted away, replaced by an almost supernatural calm.

"Waters. I knew you come looking for me."

"I was worried about you, friend. Had a little run-in with the Royal Police this morning. Figured if they were after me, they might come looking for you." Mark gestured with his hands and looked around the room. "But, obviously you're not too concerned. Not enough to stop chasing underage tail, anyway."

Lau spat on the floor in front of Mark. "You still don't get it, stupid farrang! I not your friend. I was your partner. I with you to make money!"

Mark lurched forward and grabbed Lau by the lapels of his colorful shirt.

"We were making money, you stupid bastard! What the hell did you do?"

Lau glared at him. "We making peanuts. You wasting my time. You too scared to take the next step, so I take it for you!"

Mark slammed his fist into Lau's gut and dropped the coughing, sputtering man to the ground.

"Why are the Royal Police all over this? Why are they so worked up over a bunch of counterfeit purses and designer jeans?"

Lau wiped his mouth with his arm and glared up at Mark.

"Not jeans, asshole. Not this time. Something bigger. Your bribe too small now. You no longer protected."

Mark took a step towards Lau's prostrate body. He kept his voice low, but even with the thumping music outside, his words cut through the room like a blade of ice.

"Drugs?"

Lau laughed, a short, pained bark, and propped himself up to a sitting position on the floor.

"Not drugs. Guns."

Does it matter? Mark wondered. He knew both charges carried the death penalty.

"How did the police find them?"

Lau shrugged. "I tell them, of course. I change the shipment. I inform Chief Battang of the new arrangement. He get to make big arrest for gun smuggling. Now that you out of picture, he get bigger cut for future shipments."

Mark stared at the man in shock. "You told him? You burned an entire shipment of guns just to sell me out?"

"Could have burned two ... three, fuck it! Money well spent. You think too small. We have the contacts; we have boat. The police are in our pocket. We making pennies when we could have big score! Drugs, guns, women! This my operation now. Consider this your retirement!"

In the space of a heartbeat, between the pulses of laser light, Mark's anger burned into white-hot fury. His mouth twisted in a silent snarl.

Lau gasped in fear and tried to shield himself with his hands. Mark grabbed him by his shirt, hoisted him into the air, and threw him back against the wall with all his strength.

He pummeled Lau's pudgy face, first in a series of measured, one-two strikes. But soon the punches became more erratic. Each wild swing battered Lau's flesh with a dull thud.

"You have no idea!" Mark screamed. "No idea what you've done! You hear me, you piece of shit?"

Mark's fist rose to strike again, when he felt a sudden blunt impact on the back of his head. He dropped to the ground as more blows rained down on his body. Several Royal Police had stormed the room; in his rage, Mark had left his back to the door.

One of the officers helped Lau to his feet. The traitor could barely stand, but he pushed the officer away from him. He grabbed a white towel from a bottle of champagne in the corner to wipe the blood from his mangled face.

He knelt down in front of Mark.

"I know exactly what I did, farrang. I did what you afraid to do. You don't belong here anymore. You never did."

Lau stood back up and took a long, hard look at Mark, who was moaning and rolling on the floor. His leg shot out, kicking Mark in the face. The force of the blow rolled Mark onto his back. He stared up at the blurred faces of Lau and the policemen.

A lone thought went through Mark's mind before he slipped into unconsciousness. After he was arrested, the name "Mark Waters," along with his fingerprints, would be processed through Interpol's computers. The results would show up on the daily logs of every intelligence service in the Western world.

That was going to cause problems since his name was not, in fact, Mark Waters.

It was Thomas Caine.

To keep reading, get Tokyo Black at Amazon now…

THANK YOU!

Thank you for reading *Depth Charge*. If you enjoyed this novella, would you please consider leaving an honest review for it at Amazon? Reviews are critical for helping independent authors bring their books to the attention of readers who might enjoy them. I would truly appreciate it, and it can be as short as you like.

If you would like to learn more about me and my books, please visit my website, andrewwarrenbooks.com, or my Facebook page.

Thank you very much.

AAW

THE THOMAS CAINE SERIES

Thank you for reading *Depth Charge*. If you enjoyed this novella, here are some other books featuring betrayed assassin Thomas Caine...

CAINE: RAPID FIRE SERIES

DEVIL'S DUE

Caine: Rapid Fire Book 1

COLD KILL

Caine: Rapid Fire Book 2

SANDFIRE

Caine: Rapid Fire Book 3

DEPTH CHARGE

Caine: Rapid Fire Book 4

THOMAS CAINE NOVELS

TOKYO BLACK

A Thomas Caine Thriller

RED PHOENIX

A Thomas Caine Thriller

FIRE AND FORGET

A Thomas Caine Thriller

ALSO BY AIDEN L. BAILEY

BLOOD IVORY
A Simon Ashcroft Novella

THE ASSYRIAN CONTRABAND
A Simon Ashcroft Novella

THE BENEVOLENT DECEPTION
A Simon Ashcroft Thriller

THOMAS CAINE
will
RETURN!

Please Join my Readers Group!

You might get a chance to read the next Thomas Caine thriller for free! You'll also get access to special sales, contests, and new release info...

Please visit
AndrewWarrenbooks.com
for more details.
Thank you.

ACKNOWLEDGMENTS

The authors wish to extend our thanks to Bob Adamcik (LCDR USN, retired) and friends for unclassified insights on submarine capabilities. We would also like to thank Samuel Carver for providing background information on the culture, geography and politics of China, Hong Kong and Macau. To paraphrase Stephen King, what we got right is thanks to them. What we got wrong is thanks to us.

Special thanks must go to Bodo Pfündl, the 'Typo Assassin', for his lethal proof-reading skills.

Finally, a big thank you to all our readers... without you, none of this would be possible!

THANK YOU.

ANDREW WARREN

Andrew Warren was born in New Jersey, and studied film, English, and psychology at the University of Miami. He has over a decade of experience in the television and motion picture industry, where he has worked as a post production supervisor, story producer, and writer. He currently lives in Southern California.

Andrew loves to hear from his readers! Please feel free to contact him here:

www.andrewwarrenbooks.com
andrew@andrewwarrenbooks.com

AIDEN L. BAILEY

Formerly an engineer, Aiden L Bailey built a career marketing multinational technology, heavy industry and construction companies. His various roles have included corporate communications with the Australian Submarine Corporation, technical writing for several defense contractors, engineering on a petroleum pipeline constructed in the Australian desert, and a magazine editor and art director. He travelled widely in his twenties, predominately through Australia, Africa, Europe and South America, and returned home with many stories to tell. Aiden lives with his wife and daughter in South Australia.

To learn more, visit Aiden's website at aidenlbailey.com

Join Aiden's Readers Group and and receive a FREE Thriller. To join, visit aidenlbailey.com.